The Search for the

Crystal Key

Ellyn Dye

BLUE LION
PRESS

THE SEARCH FOR THE CRYSTAL KEY.
Copyright © 2008 Ellyn Dye

Map by Jonathan Horstman.

ISBN: 978-0-6152-3553-0

Printed in the United States of America.

For EMILY

And for all the others who have
amazing powers they haven't discovered yet

And
in loving memory
of some of my own Wise Ones:
Mora Plager Dye
Jessie Blackburn
Norman James

Who's Who

At Home

Sam — Frankie's little brother.

Aunt Cassie — Frankie's favorite aunt, her father's sister, who has been mysteriously ill for a long time.

In Alaris

Aldebaran (Al-da-bear-an) — A Unicorn.

Aldreth (All-dreth) — Ilayna's father, son of Unarius, married to Aradia, he died when Janra tried to conquer Alaris.

Cassandra (Ka-san-dra) — A woman from another world who came to Alaris hundreds of years ago, she studied under Cybele with Belzar and is said to have disappeared following a great battle with Belzar.

Cybele (Sib-el) — One of the Old Wise Ones, a Crystal Master of Alaris, and the Guardian of the Doors Between Worlds, she was the teacher of Belzar and Cassandra hundreds of years ago. The subject of legends and folklore, she is said to have disappeared around the time of the battle between Belzar and Cassandra.

Ilayna (I-lay-na) — The niece of the warrior queen, Janra; daughter of Janra's sister, Aradia; and the granddaughter of Unarius, she is Frankie's age, studying herbology and crystal lore under Uriel.

Sebastian (Se-bast-ee-an) — A big orange cat living with Uriel.

Uriel (Your-ee-el) — One of the Wise Ones of Alaris, she is teaching Ilayna herbology and crystal lore.

Unarius (You-nair-ee-us) — The Crystal Master and one of the Wise Ones of Alaris, he is Ilayna's grandfather, Aradia's father-in-law, and Frankie's teacher.

In Kelghard Fortress

Aldrid (All-drid) — A girl who works in Kelghard Fortress, imprisoned by Janra on charges of spying for Aradia.

Aradia (Ah-ray-dee-ah) — Sister of warrior queen Janra and mother of Ilayna, she was married to the son of Unarius, Aldreth, who died during Janra's attempt to conquer Alaris.

Belzar (Bell-zar) — A long-ago ancestor of Janra, who studied with Cassandra under Cybele and died following a legendary battle with Cassandra. She was the first ruler of Kelghard to try to conquer Alaris.

Daisy — Ilayna's horse.

Jamie — Stable boy at Kelghard, he is Ilayna's friend.

Janra — (Zhan-ra) — Queen of Kelghard, a descendant of Belzar, she is the first ruler of Kelghard since Belzar to try to conquer Alaris.

Janra's Men:
> **Caius** (Ky-us)
> **Darius** (Dar-ee-us)
> **Malus** (Mal-us)

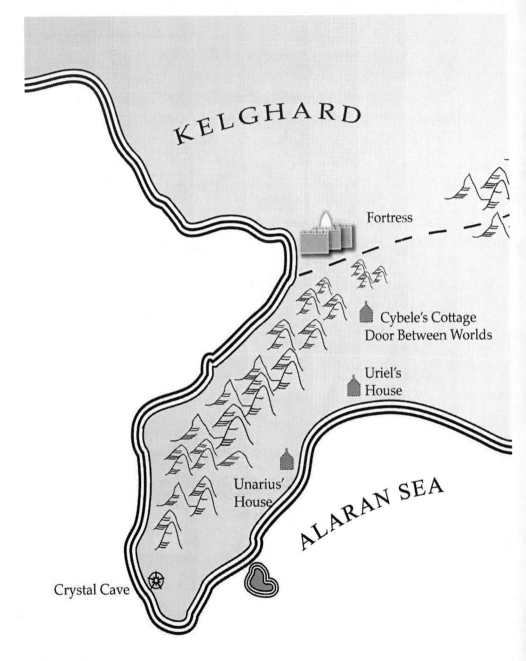

KELGHARD

Fortress

Cybele's Cottage
Door Between Worlds

Uriel's
House

Unarius'
House

ALARAN SEA

Crystal Cave

Prologue

The Dream

There was nothing Frankie Maxwell could do but sit on the old split-rail fence, spellbound, and watch the two women fight in the clearing in front of her. Actually, she didn't *want* to do anything else—she just wanted to stay well out of the way. But she couldn't tear her eyes away and she didn't want to miss anything.

The woman on the huge white unicorn lunged forward, standing up in her stirrups. She heaved what looked like a long ice spear at the other woman, who jerked back the reins of her giant black stallion to avoid being hit.

As the spear flew toward its rider, the stallion snorted, bared its teeth, reared back on its hind legs, and spun around to the right. He landed with such force that the earth shuddered, sending Frankie flying backwards off the fence. She scrambled back up as fast as she could and wrapped her arms around a tree to hold herself steady.

Bolts of orange and purple lightning punctuated the cold gray fog, which swirled into the clearing and hung like spider webs in the branches of the ancient trees. The trees huddled in around the edges of the clearing as if they, too, were afraid to miss something. The warriors' muttered oaths, their heated breath, and the wheezing snorts of their steeds hung frozen in the cold foggy air.

Frankie's hair stood up on end and she shivered all over. Her mother used to say that a spine-tingling shiver meant that someone was walking on your grave. This time, Frankie believed it. She moved her arms for a tighter grip on the tree.

The black stallion and the white unicorn circled each other. The horse neighed and snorted, rolling its wide eyes in terror. The unicorn nudged its pointed silver horn closer and closer to the horse's neck. The two beasts lunged, retreated, and circled around in a kind of dance, as their riders jockeyed for position and tried to find a vulnerable spot to hit with dagger or spear.

The women looked like ancient Amazon warriors with their sturdy and worn leather garments, heavy shields, and spears. Bows and quivers of arrows hung strapped across their chests. Too close to use the bows, they fought for their lives in hand-to-hand combat, gripping their steeds with their knees. They stabbed and gouged with long knives, and pushed against each other with their shields. They grabbed and twisted handfuls of hair escaping from under leather helmets in the heat of battle, as each desperately tried to pull the other off her mount, to get the upper hand.

The women were well matched, and each time one gained a hold or landed a blow, the other balanced it with one of her own. The battle had raged for hours and the warriors and their steeds were wounded and weary.

There was a final crack of steel-upon-steel, and the horse and unicorn leaped away from each other and stopped suddenly, snorting and pawing the ground.

"You think you've won, Cassandra, but you haven't," shouted the warrior on the black stallion in a mean, grating voice. Her hair was as black and thick as her horse's mane. It hung down in loose strands that clung in clumps to the sweat on her face and neck. She watched the other woman so intently that she didn't seem to notice the long bleeding gash down her left side or the purple bruises swelling on her face. "I'm not finished with you yet!" she shouted. "I'll see to it that you'll wish you'd never been born—in my world *or* yours!"

"Ha!" yelled the other woman, who wheezed and gasped as raggedly as the unicorn she rode, "you don't believe that! You have to defeat me and many others in order to win. As long as the Light penetrates the Darkness even a little bit, you haven't won. And you won't win, because I will keep coming back for you, and others will join me. We will defeat you, Belzar! You have made the wrong choice. You have used your skills for evil, and you and your kind will pay the price!"

The unicorn pranced backward as the copper-haired Cassandra lowered her sword and pointed it toward Belzar and her black horse. But before they could lunge forward and strike, Belzar summoned up her remaining strength and stood up in her stirrups. She flung her hand out toward her enemy with a final burst of energy. Orange sparks flew like lightning from her fingertips, sizzling and sputtering through the air. They hit Cassandra's sword arm before she could bring up her shield to deflect them, and the unicorn and rider were momentarily wrapped in an orange neon glow.

Cassandra threw the sword with her wounded arm before collapsing across her unicorn's neck. It flew in a wide arc, almost in slow motion. Frankie watched it finally find its target, piercing Belzar's leg and pinning it to the black stallion's side. Horse and rider went down with screams of pain and the earth shuddered again.

Cassandra and the unicorn turned slowly away from the

other wounded warrior and hobbled toward the edge of the clearing. Frankie could see their open wounds as they came closer to her seat on the fence. The unicorn's silvery white mane was tinged crimson with blood, and the woman's right arm gaped open in a long, jagged cut.

"You won't be able to sit on the fence much longer, Frankie Maxwell," the warrior said as she drew up next to her. "You are part of this, you know, and soon you will have to take a stand." She closed her eyes and was so still that Frankie was afraid that the woman had passed out. But she opened her eyes again and continued.

"I'm wounded badly and it will be a long time before I will be able to come back and finish this fight. But there is too much to lose and we must continue. It may be your turn sooner than you think."

Frankie knew this woman, and the crest on the front of her leather vest looked familiar. But Frankie couldn't bring to mind who she was. As she craned her neck to watch the warrior and the unicorn move slowly out of the clearing and into the deep ancient forest, Frankie lost her balance again, fell backwards off the fence, and landed on the ground with a thump.

♥　　♥　　♥

Frankie woke up with a start, still feeling that awful falling sensation, as if the world had been jerked out from under her. She grabbed frantically at the covers to steady herself. She was sweaty and chilled all over, and she had the terrible feeling that those warriors and angry beasts had been fighting their battle in the middle of her very own bedroom. She could still see wisps of that soupy gray fog in the corners of the room, and smell whiffs of ozone from purple lightning lingering in the air.

Who were those women? And why did they seem so familiar? As she stared across the room, the family pictures on her bureau caught her eye, and Frankie suddenly knew. She recognized one of them, at least. And it terrified her: Cassandra. Aunt Cassie. Her Dad's sister. She'd been really sick lately. Was she all right? It was Frankie's favorite aunt on that beautiful unicorn, and those deep bleeding wounds had certainly looked real. What if they were?

Frankie rubbed her knuckles into her eyes, trying to wake up enough to focus on the hint of an idea floating just outside her awareness. Aunt Cassie had told Frankie once about an adventure she'd had. . . something about finding her way into another world, fighting the forces of evil, being wounded badly, but escaping home to rest and recover. Frankie hadn't paid much attention to it. She'd thought it was just another of her aunt's entertaining stories, a story told to explain away her lingering illness and keep Frankie from worrying.

Now Frankie wasn't so sure. She had an unsettling feeling that her dream and Aunt Cassie's strange story and illness were linked somehow. Could the story possibly be true? Had Aunt Cassie really gone to another world? Had she really been fighting that terrifying woman warrior in that clearing? And had Frankie somehow managed to see in her dream a fight that had actually happened — *somewhere*?

Frankie pulled on a pair of heavy green socks to guard against the chill of the hardwood floors and jumped out of bed. She ran downstairs into the kitchen, shrugging her navy velour robe on over her flannel nightgown as she went. She passed her younger brother, Sam, in the living room, as he headed outside, dribbling most of an egg-and-sausage sandwich down the front of his denim overalls.

Her father looked up from washing the breakfast dishes as she skidded into the kitchen.

"Frankie, do you always have to come rocketing into a

room like the house is on fire? Running around the house is not acceptable for young ladies."

Frankie wondered briefly who cared about what young ladies did or did not do. She slid on her stocking'd feet to a halt next to the phone on the kitchen counter and perched up on a handy stool in one smooth, practiced motion.

"What's Aunt Cassie's phone number? I have to call her." She grabbed up the family phone directory and thumbed through it, but the pages were coming loose and she couldn't seem to find the right entry.

Her father dried his hands, put the dish towel down on the counter and advanced across the room toward her. "What's the matter with you? Give it here before you tear it apart." He grabbed the directory out of her hands and brandished it at her. "You're 13 now. You have to stop acting like a child."

Frankie watched him warily as she reached for one of the jelly donuts in a box on the counter. She wondered what bug had bitten *him* this morning. Maybe he'd had nightmares, too? Whatever it was, she hated it when he was like this: He acted like she was totally defective, like nothing she did was good enough, and everything she wanted to do was stupid or bad.

"Look at you. You sleep through breakfast and then gobble down donuts," her father said, slamming the phone directory down on the counter. He leaned back with his arms folded across his chest like he was really about to get into it. "Those donuts are going to go right to your hips. Maybe if you didn't eat so much junk food, you'd do better in gym class."

So *that* was it, Frankie thought. She'd gotten a *D* in gym. Gym was never one of her best classes, and she absolutely hated jogging, which had been the focus of the classes for the past six weeks. She admitted it. She was good at other things, so she didn't particularly care. But her father cared. A lot.

He apparently *didn't* care about her *A*'s in English and history. But he sure seemed to care about that *D* in gym. He'd been a star athlete in college, and he thought everyone should excel at sports. Every sport! And he'd been bringing it up for a week and hounding her about it, as if that was the only thing in the world to talk about. Knowing it would annoy him even more—but unable to stop herself, Frankie looked him straight in the eye and took a bite out of the donut in her hand. White confectioner's sugar sprinkled down the front of her navy robe.

"I know, Dad," Frankie said, swallowing a mouthful. "I'm just hungry."

"If you'd get up at a reasonable hour and eat a sensible breakfast, you wouldn't be hungry," he said, not quite making his point. He handed her a paper napkin. He leaned in toward her and she could see that he was just warming up.

"And leave your Aunt Cassie alone. You know she's been sick, and she doesn't need you bothering her. You can talk to her at your grandfather's tonight. Just go upstairs and do your chores. The last time I saw it, your room looked like a tornado hit it, and the bathroom is a disgrace. . . "

Frankie just sat on the stool and sighed, waiting for the tirade to end. What could she do? He was obviously in one of those moods again: Nothing she did was good enough. It seemed lately that in his eyes she was either totally perfect or totally useless, all or nothing, with no middle ground.

And since her mother had died of cancer last year, her father seemed to get these moods more and more often. He either ignored her or made her crazy.

Frankie tried to help around the house, to take care of Sam, to fill the terrible void and emptiness in all their lives. But nothing worked, nothing she did could make it right again. And he seemed to blame *her*. He didn't seem to understand that she missed her mom terribly, too. And when he acted like this, she felt like she was losing him, as well. Sometimes, when she just couldn't stand it anymore, she would dig her heels in and challenge him. At least she got his attention that way. But it really only made it worse.

So she did what she usually ended up doing when he was like this: She sat and held her tongue and waited until her father wandered out the door, still muttering at her under his breath.

And then she flipped through the phone directory for the number, picked up the phone, and started dialing.

1

Cassie's Story

"**I**'m so bored I could scream! Nothing ever happens! I'd do *anything* for an exciting adventure, or anything that isn't so boring, boring, boring!"

Frankie slammed her fist down emphatically on her grandparents' dining room table, then grabbed wildly to catch her glass of soda before it toppled over and completely ruined the linen tablecloth. The Thanksgiving dishes were cleared away and everybody had scattered. Everybody except Frankie and her Aunt Cassie, who were still sitting at the table, talking.

Even though her aunt had assured her on the phone that she was fine, Frankie had felt vaguely worried all afternoon. Now that she had seen her favorite aunt and truly satisfied herself that she had not been mortally wounded in a fight on a unicorn with an Amazon warrior, Frankie was able to relax.

"I'd take being bored over being sick any day, kiddo," Aunt Cassie said, teasing her. But it really was no joke, because her aunt had a strange illness, and nobody knew what it was. It just happened one day two years ago, with no warning. Aunt Cassie was fine one day, and very sick the next.

She never had much energy anymore, and she was very pale.

Frankie sighed and hunched her shoulders forward, suddenly feeling sort of guilty about feeling bored.

Aunt Cassie assured her that she was slowly getting better, but Frankie wasn't sure she could count on that. She wasn't sure she could count on *anything* anymore. When Frankie's mother got cancer last year and died within six months, everything totally changed. Frankie's secure, predictable world had turned upside down, and nothing seemed solid, nothing seemed like it would ever last again. She could no longer trust in the goodness of the world. In fact, it had become a harsh world, where terrible, agonizing things happen, where nothing is reliable and important things can be taken away without warning.

Aunt Cassie was the only one in the family that Frankie felt she could talk to, and now Aunt Cassie was sick. What would happen if she died, too? Frankie didn't think she would be able to bear it. She really wished she could do something to help her aunt get better. Soon!

"Oh, Aunt Cassie," Frankie sighed, "I wish. . ." She stopped, looked at her aunt, and shook her head in helplessness instead of finishing her thought.

"Be careful what you wish for, my dear, you just might get it!" Aunt Cassie said, laughing and patting her arm. "You said you wanted an adventure. Is that what you really want?"

Frankie thought about it for a minute, running her finger around a little pile of salt that someone had spilled on the ivory tablecloth during dinner. She wanted *something* to happen, but she wasn't sure just what—except getting her mother back, of course, and that was impossible. But Frankie wasn't sure that she could handle a real adventure right now. It might be dangerous. And her Dad would be furious. "Well, I. . . oh, I don't know."

"Listen," Aunt Cassie said, "I wished for an adventure

once, and I kept saying I was *sick* of my life—well, I got my adventure, all right, *and* I got good and *sick*! So be careful what you ask for. The things we say and think have more power than you know!"

Frankie might not be sure about wanting an adventure, but she *was* sure that she wanted to help her aunt and said so.

"I appreciate the thought, Sweetheart," Aunt Cassie said, pulling her close in a comforting hug, "but I think it's beyond either of us to make me well any faster. And even if you could do it, I'm afraid it would take a bit more than you bargained for. . ."

"What do you mean?" Frankie asked. "Why are you sick, Aunt Cassie? What is it? It's not. . ."

Cassandra Maxwell, Frankie's Aunt Cassie, smoothed her hand over her niece's long wavy hair—copper colored and thick just like her own—and stared off into space as if she were looking at something only she could see in the thick woods outside the big picture window.

"No, Honey, it's not cancer. I promise you that. And I'm not going to die anytime soon, unless I get hit by a bus or something," she finally said. "I really am going to get well and be around for a long time. I'm not leaving you."

"Well what is it, then?"

"I told you once what it was, but you probably didn't believe me. Most people wouldn't."

"What do you mean? If you told me something, I would believe it. What was it?"

Aunt Cassie sat quietly for a moment and then sighed. "Remember when I told you I was poking around one day and I found a doorway into a different world?"

"Yeah, but. . ."

"Well, I wasn't kidding. It's really true. I went for a long visit—a real adventure—in that other world and I learned and experienced a lot of new things."

"I thought you just made that up so I wouldn't worry about you being sick," Frankie said.

"No, I told you the truth, so you'd know *why* I was sick, so you wouldn't worry." Aunt Cassie took off her necklace and handed it to Frankie.

Frankie recognized it because her aunt wore it all the time. She looked closer and saw that the medallion had a woman's face etched into it—it was a beautiful woman with long wavy hair with jewels woven into it, wearing a sort of headband across her forehead. Frankie had never really looked at it closely before, and she felt somehow that the woman in the picture was very wise and kind.

"Who's this lady, and why do you wear this necklace so often?" Frankie asked.

"This necklace means a lot to me. . . and it reminds me of where I've been and what I know," Aunt Cassie said. "It's a sort of graduation present. No, it's more like a portable diploma. There were only two of these made at the time—one is mine, the other one belonged to another woman who studied with me. We both studied with the woman on the necklace for years. Her name was Cybele and she was very wise. She taught us all about herbs and energy and crystals and all kinds of things."

"It doesn't sound like an adventure to me," Frankie said, carefully putting the necklace down on the table. "It just sounds like school. And even though school makes me sick, it couldn't have really made *you* sick!"

Aunt Cassie laughed but quickly became serious again. "Well, it wasn't all school. I got sick because something went wrong and I had to leave in a hurry," she said. "But in my rush to get back home I sort of left part of myself there. Part of the very essence of myself, part of the core of my Being. Does that make any sense to you?"

"I guess so," Frankie said, sounding dubious. "I could

understand if you got hurt and lost a finger or something." She shuddered at the thought. "But I'm not sure what you mean about Essence. I mean, you're here, aren't you?"

Aunt Cassie held up her arm and pinched it. "Yes, I'm physically here. But we're so much more than our physical bodies. We have an essence, a spirit, a soul—whatever you want to call it. That's what animates our bodies. It's our Divine spark, our vitality. Our connection to the Creator. It's who we are."

She took a sip of water, smoothed the table cloth with her hand, and stared out the window for a minute without speaking.

"I think I get it," Frankie ventured. "Was it a particular part of you that you left there? Does essence have parts?"

Aunt Cassie looked puzzled, as if she'd never thought of that before. "You know, I think it may have been a specific part. I think I left the part that empowers me: the inner strength that prompts me to stand up for myself and fight when I need to." She paused again, with a strange look on her face, and then continued. "Yes, I think that's it, if anything. I've lost my fight. That's an important part of all of us, and I can't seem to call it up to fight off this strange illness."

Then she shook off whatever had come over her. "But the main thing is, Frankie, I don't have all of my Essence here. Part of me is split off, so I'm not whole, and I don't have all my usual vitality."

"So when Dad says you're 'not all there' sometimes—you really *aren't* all here?" Frankie was surprised to think the cliché might have some truth to it.

Aunt Cassie laughed. "That's exactly it! He says it as a joke, but he's right! And I won't be *all here* until I can go *back there* and get that missing part of me back. I just have to get my strength back first, and that will take awhile. But you don't have to worry about me. I *will* get better—in time."

"Have you told Dad that you have to go get that part of you? He could probably do something." Frankie might not be particularly happy with her father these days, but she figured he could fix just about anything.

Aunt Cassie laughed again. "I'm afraid not, Frankie. Your Dad decided I was nuts before I even finished telling him. He thought it was just a stupid story I made up, and he couldn't believe I could possibly think that's why I've been sick." She shook her head sadly, and Frankie felt bad for her—she knew what it was like to have her Dad scoff and refuse to believe what you're telling him.

"So when he says that I'm 'not all there,' he means that my mental capacities are faulty! That I'm crazy! I tried to tell the family why I was sick, and they almost had me committed!" She sighed.

"But why wouldn't they believe you?" Frankie asked, conveniently forgetting that she hadn't really believed her, either.

"They thought my story was crazy because it was too far outside their view of reality for them to accept. But I can tell you, Frankie, there's a lot more 'reality' out there than most people think!" Aunt Cassie shook off her sadness like an old, familiar sweater.

"But really, Frankie. Whatever the cause of this strange illness of mine, I am absolutely sure that I'll be fine. You really don't have to worry. It really is just a matter of time. I'm not going anywhere. I will be here for you. I promise. I'll be here for me, too!"

Frankie thought about that for a minute and suddenly had a wild thought that made her skin crawl. A shiver ran down her spine as she asked, "Aunt Cassie, when you say, 'Something went wrong,' what do you mean?"

Aunt Cassie looked a little surprised, but told her anyway. "Actually, I got in kind of a fight. . ."

"A sword fight, with a woman on a huge black horse, with you riding a unicorn?" Frankie asked, all in a rush.

Aunt Cassie whistled long and low. "How in the world did you know that?"

Frankie hadn't told her about her dream, because she was afraid it would sound stupid. But with her aunt's prompting, she told her.

"I don't know what to say, Frankie," she said. "That fight happened just as you dreamed it—but you weren't there, of course. Belzar and I trained together and we were pretty evenly matched. It's a shame she chose the Dark path. I don't know why you had that dream or what it means. But dreams are always important and it probably means something."

Frankie suddenly jumped up, feeling a little scared, but sure that her idea was the right thing to do. "I could help you! I could go there and get that part of you back! In my dream, you *told me* I would have to get involved, that it's time for me to do something!"

"OH NO YOU CAN'T!" Aunt Cassie jumped up, too. She grabbed Frankie by the shoulders and squeezed hard. "Frankie, I mean this seriously. Don't make me sorry I told you, please. It's too dangerous. Why do you think I need to get back my strength first? I don't know what it will be like there when I go back, and there's no telling what kind of danger I might fall into. So I'm certainly not going to let *you* go!"

"But you said it was wonderful there!"

"Honey, it *was* wonderful! But then it changed. When I left, I was running from the bad guys, fleeing for my life! And it might not be so wonderful now. A lot can happen over time, especially there: Time passes faster there than it does here. I was there for years, but when I got back here, no time had passed. It's been two years here since I came back, so it could have been hundreds of years there. It's got to be very different now. Things just don't stay the same. They always change.

And in this case, the changes might be very bad. I hope not, but it's possible."

Aunt Cassie relaxed her grip, and Frankie was sure that there would be red impressions on her shoulders where her aunt's fingers had been.

"But in my dream," she protested, "you said it was my turn to join the fight! You *had* to mean that I should go there!"

"No, Frankie, that was probably just symbolic," Aunt Cassie said, gently patting Frankie's left shoulder, where her fingers had been. "Dreams are like that! But listen to me now. I mean this, more than anything I've ever told you: DON'T EVEN *THINK* ABOUT GOING THERE! I would die from worry!"

"Okay, okay." Frankie said, pushing herself away and absently rubbing her other shoulder. She was a little confused. Her aunt had never spoken to her in that tone of voice before—that was *Dad's* serious tone—and Frankie knew she meant business. But Frankie also knew that this was the first time since her mother died that she felt like maybe she could actually *do* something to help, instead of just standing by, helpless, as something terrible happened. And she wanted to help her aunt get well more than anything she had wanted in a long, long time.

The mood was shattered, suddenly, by Frankie's father's booming voice, coming from the den.

"FRANKIE! What are you doing in there?"

"NOTHING!" Frankie and her aunt answered in unison, then laughed quietly at each other.

"Leave your aunt alone. She's not well." He shouted.

"Okay, Dad," Frankie hollered back.

"See what I mean?" Aunt Cassie said, rolling her eyes and quoting: "She's not well!" Suddenly serious again, she went on. "But look, Frankie, I really mean it. There's no way you can go there. I know it's really hard to just stand by and do nothing, but there's really nothing you can do." She gave her niece a quick, strong hug. "Let's go into the den and see what's up—unless you want to go downstairs and play with the kids? I won't be offended if you find them more fun than the grownups."

"No, I don't want to go downstairs," Frankie said, a little disappointed, but also slightly relieved, that her aunt opposed her plan. It probably *was* a little crazy.

"They're just chasing each other around and screaming. . . of course, all they're doing in the den is watching the football game and screaming, and that's just as bad. I hate football!"

"Me, too," Aunt Cassie said, holding her finger to her lips as if it were a deep, dark secret, "but don't tell anybody! It's sacrilegious to hate football in this family! Let's just hope they only have it on as background noise. But I'm feeling a little tired, kiddo, and I can stretch out on the sofa in there and rest a little. . ."

Frankie suddenly noticed how pale her aunt looked, and she was afraid her questions had somehow caused it or made it worse.

She picked up the necklace from the table and started to follow her aunt into the den. But then she stopped and stood listening to the various noises in this big rambling house that belonged to her grandparents—the house where her Dad and Aunt Cassie grew up. It was a comfortable place, filled with old, familiar, comfortable things, comfortable smells, comfortable noises. It was one of the few places where Frankie still felt safe and secure. This was a place where things *didn't* change. It was a place she could count on.

A great noise rumbled up from the basement, where her brother and six of their cousins were running around, in and out of the rooms, chasing each other, playing monsters and warriors, and generally acting like kids. They weren't so bad, really, but they were still just kids. And Frankie, at 13, was not a kid anymore. At least part of her wasn't. Most of her. Sometimes. Or something. Every once in awhile, though, she'd have a sudden urge to grab someone's toy and run screaming down the hall with the rest of them.

But other times she felt like she'd never be young again. From the top of the stairs she wistfully watched the group of kids shrieking and yelling at each other, having a terrific time. She felt so in-between sometimes, as if she really didn't fit anywhere. And most of the time, she felt restless and bored and filled with anticipation, as if something huge was about to happen, but hadn't yet. And no one seemed to understand how she felt, except Aunt Cassie.

Frankie sighed and, with a last look toward the basement stairs and the kids, she walked toward the den and the grownups. A debate raged in one corner of the small cozy room about some political thing, but it was drowned out by cheering for a touch-down on television from the other side of the room.

Frankie hovered in the doorway, and Aunt Cassie looked up and smiled and waved, patting the empty seat cushion next to her on the sofa. Frankie crossed the room and sat down next to her aunt, struck again by how alike they were. Her aunt wore her wavy copper hair shorter than Frankie did, but the dark blue eyes, slender nose, and fair complexion were the same. And it was not just looks, either. Frankie always felt that the two of them were alike inside, too. They saw things the same way, felt the same things. It felt as if somehow they had known each other forever, beyond this time and space.

"I thought we'd lost you," Aunt Cassie said. "Are you having trouble deciding between the adults and the kids?"

Frankie nodded and plucked absently at the green wool afghan that was tucked around her aunt's legs.

"I know how you feel," her aunt continued, "but I'm afraid that feeling of being in-between isn't something that you completely outgrow—even as a grownup there are times when you'll feel like you don't quite fit in anywhere. I feel that way sometimes, too."

Frankie couldn't believe that, because her Aunt Cassie always seemed to fit in perfectly everywhere she went.

"It's sad but true, kiddo," Aunt Cassie told her, as if she read her mind, "although feeling that way might not be such a bad thing, even if it feels uncomfortable. I'll tell you a secret: The more you get to know *and be* who you really are, deep inside—and the less you try to be like everybody else and fit in—the less awkward you feel. Because then you feel at home with YOU, wherever you are."

"But how long does that take?" Frankie asked.

Aunt Cassie laughed. "Oh, my, it takes some people forever! And if it doesn't actually take that long, it can feel like it does! But truly, if you just follow that little voice inside that knows who you really are, you'll get there."

Frankie didn't find that particularly comforting. She suddenly remembered she had picked up the necklace and she held it out to her aunt.

"It's nice, isn't it?" Aunt Cassie asked, and Frankie nodded. "I don't really feel like wearing it right now, though. Sometimes it just feels awfully heavy, if you know what I mean. Would you do me a favor and put it in my purse for me? It's on the bed with all the coats in the back bedroom. You know, the one that used to be mine?"

Frankie smiled and nodded, her fingers curling once again around the necklace. She got up and headed for the hall.

2

An Unusual Portrait

Frankie opened the door to the back bedroom and saw the coats and handbags piled up on the big bed. This had always been her favorite room in the house, because it had been Aunt Cassie's and it still seemed to bear her aunt's mark. It had always seemed to be magic or enchanted somehow, although Frankie couldn't put her finger on exactly why.

She loved the large four-poster bed and the brass lamp in the shape of a wizard holding a lantern that sat on the small bedside stand.

She also loved the knickknacks that sat on a purple fringed scarf on the chest of drawers: A crystal bell with a smoky glass butterfly perched on top; a graceful brass candlestick with a dark purple, partly burned candle still in it; a small silver Revere bowl like the larger one they had on top of the china cabinet at home, filled with potpourri that smelled like cinnamon; and a long slender rod of clear stone that looked as much like a magic wand as anything Frankie had ever seen. She wondered if that was really what it was and why her aunt

would have left it—or any of the other magical things—
behind. As Frankie had done countless times before over the
years, she reached her hand out toward it, then drew it back,
not quite wanting to touch it to find out if it was really magic
or not.

Frankie looked the other items over very carefully, picking
each one up, feeling its texture and testing its weight, and
returned each one to its place. It was a ritual she performed
every time she visited her grandparents' house.

She moved on to the bookcase, which was half-filled with
dusty books with interesting titles like *The Energy of Gems and
Crystals, The Lost City of Atlantis,* and *The Human Energy Field.*
These books were much more interesting than the musty old
National Geographic magazines and murder mysteries on the
shelves at home. She'd often wondered what they were about,
but had never gotten around to asking her aunt.

She turned to the night stand, which held the brass wizard
lamp. It sported a small silver clock that showed the time as
7:06 p.m. and a calendar with a view of the earth from outer
space showing the date. It seemed odd that the date would be
right on a calendar in a guest room. Someone must have fixed
it.

After inspecting everything very carefully, Frankie went
over to the big mirror standing in the corner. At least six feet
tall, the mirror was held in a massive, heavily carved wooden
stand that stood even taller. The stand had big, clawed feet
and fat poles with vines carved up around them, and carved
pineapples at the top. Sometimes, if Frankie looked at those
poles out of the corner of her eye, it seemed that she could
almost see those carved vines growing and moving around the
poles, as if they were real and alive. And she would swear she
had seen images of magic lands in other dimensions when she
looked at that mirror *just so.*

The only thing in the room that was more interesting than

the mirror was a larger-than-life portrait of a woman on the wall next to it. It dominated the room and seemed to be out of proportion to the other decorations. The woman had red wavy hair like Frankie's and a woven headband with a jewel of some kind in it across her forehead. She was dressed in leather garments like the ones worn by the women in Frankie's dream, but she was only shown from the waist up. The woman's figure took up so much of the canvas that it was hard to tell where she was supposed to be, but Frankie could make out a few trees in the background. There was something very commanding about the woman's bright blue eyes, and her lips turned up ever so slightly in a secretive smile.

Frankie had always liked her, feeling a strange kind of kinship with her. But she didn't know who she was or why the portrait was here. As Frankie was growing up, she loved to come to this room and pay her respects to this strangely familiar woman and make up wild stories about her. Suddenly, Frankie wondered if any of those stories that had popped into her head might actually have been true.

The frame around the portrait was dark wood as wide as Frankie's hand with her fingers splayed out. It was heavily carved in patterns of swirls and knots. Not for the first time, Frankie wondered why the frame was so massive and ornate. In another room, the portrait and frame might seem overly large and out of place. But it fit, somehow, in this room. Its very oddness added to the air of magic and enchantment.

Suddenly remembering her errand, Frankie turned to the bed, which was piled high with coats and scarves and gloves and purses. She pushed Aunt Meg's bright green coat out of the way, moved a blue and white diaper bag, and uncovered Aunt Cassie's purse.

She looked down once again at the necklace in her hand and noticed that there were strange characters on the back, etched in two lines into the metal. Frankie closed her eyes and wished it were a magic necklace that held the secret to finding that other world Aunt Cassie had talked about. She would like to be there right now, away from her Dad's temper, on her way to saving her aunt. She sighed. Maybe if she put the necklace on and said a few magic words. . . but she knew her aunt wouldn't tell her what the words were, even if there were some.

She turned it over in her hand and looked again at the woman's face. She suddenly realized that the woman on the medallion was the same as the one in the portrait. She held the necklace up to compare the two, and she was surprised to see that the portrait seemed different from before. Now she could see down to the woman's knees, and she could see the forest around her and a cottage behind her at the end of a lane. It was very odd. Frankie looked again at the big carved frame.

As her eye traced the carvings down the sides, she noticed that the bottom piece of the frame contained colored stones, sunk into it about five inches apart. She had to bend over to see them, because the bottom of the frame was about knee-high off the floor. There were five stones in different shapes and colors: a round black stone, a square light green stone, a triangular purple stone, an oval stone in palest blue, and a pink heart-shaped stone. Next to that, at the far right end of the line, there was a hole in the shape of a stop sign, but the stone that went there was missing. She wondered what color that stone had been and what had happened to it

As Frankie leaned over to look at them more closely, the pink heart-shaped stone in the frame started to glow right at her.

Without thinking, she reached down and touched it, ever so lightly. It fell off the frame and into her hand.

"Oh, my gosh! I broke it!" She dropped it, as if it had burned her palm, and she jumped back several feet, looking around to see if anyone had seen what happened.

She lost her grip on Aunt Cassie's necklace as she jumped, and she was astonished to see it fly through the air right at the picture as if it were returning to the woman pictured there. Even more astonishing, the necklace did not stop and bounce off when it hit the canvas—it kept on going. In fact, it went right into the portrait and disappeared.

Frankie rubbed her eyes, shook her head, and decided to pretend for the moment that she had not seen that happen. She looked at the portrait and it seemed to have changed again. Now, she could see the woman's full figure, walking in soft tan leather breeches and brown boots up the lane away from a rustic cottage. Frankie rubbed her eyes again and decided she would pretend she hadn't seen that, either.

"What's going on?" she asked out loud of no one in particular. She had not only lost her aunt's favorite necklace, but she also seemed to be hallucinating!

She looked down on the floor for the pink heart-shaped stone, and breathed an audible sigh of relief when she found it lying on the floor in front of her. At least that was still here! She picked up the stone, determined to put it back into the frame. But as she held it, it got warmer in her hand, and it glowed brighter and brighter, like a big, pink, blinking Christmas tree light.

And as she leaned down to put it back in the frame, as her ear was almost flat against the picture, she thought she heard a soft whisper: "Hello? Hello? Are you there? Is that you, Cassandra? The medallion has come home. Are you coming, too?"

Frankie leaped back away from the picture, staring up at it. The woman seemed to be smiling at her. She leaned in again, slowly. . . quietly, holding her breath. . . and heard it again. The voice was very soft, and Frankie could barely make out the words. But she knew there was definitely a voice, and it was definitely coming from the picture!

With the warm pink stone throbbing in her tightly clenched hand, Frankie walked backwards a few feet to get a really full view of the portrait. The woman had moved farther back up the path and was beckoning to Frankie to follow. One hand seemed to be holding Aunt Cassie's necklace. The other hand was stretched out toward Frankie, and it looked like it was coming right off the canvas into the room to grab her!

No, way! Frankie snatched her own hands behind her back for safe keeping. This was crazy! She had to be imagining things!

Frankie moved back to the portrait for another look. She could feel the frame nudging her shins and she could see the grainy texture of the oil paint. She brought her hand up and touched the canvas gingerly. It seemed to ripple and move under her fingers and the picture seemed to blur. She flattened her hand out against it to make it stop moving, to make it return to normal, to be stubbly and textured and firm again, like oil paintings are supposed to be.

But as she pushed, her hand just sank up to her wrist into the picture. Impossible! Horrified and disbelieving, yet totally unable to stop herself, she pushed her hand ever so slightly forward. And she watched, with her mouth falling open, as her hand and arm disappeared into the portrait up to the elbow!

And before she even had time to think twice about it, she was leaning forward, losing her balance, and following her hand. She gained momentum, her feet flew out from under her, and she plunged headlong into the portrait.

3

A Grumpy Unicorn

She fell into a sort of in-between place that felt like neither earth nor sky. It felt mostly like a thick fog—almost thick enough to cushion her fall, almost thick enough for her to grab in great handfuls. Almost, but not quite. It reminded Frankie of the place in her dream, that cold foggy place, but she didn't see Aunt Cassie or any warriors. She didn't see anyone or anything. She just kept falling and thinking how strange and silly and totally unbelievable it was. After all, things like this just do not happen in real life. Falling into portraits, for heaven's sake! Totally ridiculous! Besides that, her Dad would be furious!

Frankie landed with a thud, a roll, and a crashing halt that knocked the wind right out of her. She gasped for breath and reached out with her hands for the feel of something hard and stable under her. It was hard all right—she was sprawled out, face down, on a hardwood floor. And a dusty hardwood floor, at that. She could feel her nose start to twitch from the dust. But she didn't dare look. She had almost convinced herself that this was some sort of after-Thanksgiving-Dinner hallucination or something—brought on by too many of

Granddad's candied sweet potatoes or too much of Grandma's pumpkin pie. But what if it wasn't? What if it was real?

"Are you quite finished?" a gruff, impatient voice spoke from nearby. "What a production you humans make of everything! Get up, dust yourself off, and come on. We have a long way to go."

Frankie rolled over, sat up and forced herself to open her eyes. She warily looked around and found herself to be in a warm, friendly cottage. She was in the living room and she could see the kitchen area off to one side and a hallway leading to other rooms to the other side. She couldn't figure out where the voice had come from. Slowly she got up, brushed herself off, and looked around. Her first thought was to find the way back.

A huge portrait on the back wall caught her eye and she walked over to inspect it. It was the largest decoration in the room and it dominated most of the wall. Even stranger, it was a portrait of the same woman in the portrait she had just fallen through—and this time she looked like she was standing in Aunt Cassie's bedroom! Like the other one, this picture only showed the woman from the waist up, larger than life. But Frankie could just make out in the background the carved poles topped with pineapples on the mirror stand in her aunt's room. She had half expected to find that woman in the cabin. She couldn't decide if that would have been weirder than seeing her in this second portrait. Either way, it was all entirely too weird!

Frankie suddenly sneezed three times, then spun around in astonishment when she heard a gruff old voice say "Bless you" from behind. What she saw was even stranger than the portrait.

There was a small white horse standing in the doorway. But it was not really a horse, because Frankie could see a golden horn growing right out of its forehead. Frankie gasped.

It was a unicorn! And it was really beautiful—it was shimmery and white, whiter than sun on snow, or ice cream, or even her mother's white kitchen curtains fresh out of the washer. He was so glaringly white that she could see him better when she half closed her eyes, looked sideways, and squinted at him. The whiteness shimmered and moved as if it would disappear if she touched it.

And the horn! It was such a bright gold that she could barely stand to look at it at all. Maybe this was all part of that other dream? He wasn't as big and fierce as the unicorn in her dream, but he was still a unicorn. Maybe she had never awakened at all?

"I am not a dream, you silly human!" the creature said as he slowly grew to the size of a large horse, then seemed to change his mind and got smaller again. "You are looking at me, are you not? You see me, do you not? Why do I always have to go through this with people?" He stamped his small silver hoof on the ground and snorted. "How would you feel if people looked straight at you and did not believe you existed?" He sounded pretty annoyed.

Frankie shrank back instinctively against his outburst, but she agreed that she would probably find it annoying, too. But she still wasn't one hundred percent certain that she was actually seeing him. And even if he *was* a unicorn, surely he couldn't be talking!

"You can bet your life it is annoying. And you wonder why unicorns do not appear very often? *This* is why—because whenever we do, silly humans like you disbelieve us into going away. The force of disbelief is very uncomfortable. Actually it can be quite painful. So we naturally do not like to stay in that energy longer than we have to. We prefer the sweet energy of places where we are believed, not to mention actually appreciated. So if you keep up that disbelief you are feeling, I'll be going. . ."

He shimmered, and the whiteness faded until he was not much more than a faint outline, like the shimmer of heat rising off a hot road. Frankie could see right through him.

"Don't go!" Frankie screamed as she lunged out to grab a bit of silky mane before it faded away completely. "I *do* believe in unicorns. I *do* believe in you. I promise! Ask anybody!"

He started to get solid again, and he seemed to lose control of his size for a minute — as he became more solid he got small, then huge, then small again. It was almost as if he was trying to decide what size to be.

"It's just that I never saw a unicorn in person before," she added, hoping to explain her lapse into doubt, "and everybody says you don't really exist, you know. Even when you're here, you're kind of hard to see."

He flickered momentarily, then solidified once and for all with a little quiver of his mane. He'd decided to stick with the smaller version, and now his back came up almost to her waist. Frankie was glad he'd settled on that size. She didn't think she would be able to deal with the larger, fiercer unicorn she had seen flickering in and out. Dealing with this one was hard enough.

"Grownups say we do not exist, human. Grownups who do not believe in Magic anymore, or anything they cannot prove, or anything that might be inconvenient or frightening. And to grownups, everything is frightening. It is especially hard for us in *your* world, and there are only a few of the Old Ones who stay there, trying to keep the Magic alive. But it is starting to become uncomfortable even here, where we used to be taken for granted. Do you believe in Magic, human? Not that sleight-of-hand silliness you see on your television, that is just illusion. I mean *real* Magic."

"I think I do," Frankie answered. "Can you do Magic?"

"I can do my share of Magic, human, when I see the need."

She couldn't read the look he gave her, but Frankie felt

suddenly chilled. She was afraid that she'd angered him and she wasn't sure what he would do. And she didn't want to think about what he *could* do. Maybe he wasn't a nice unicorn? He was beautiful, of course, but he was also wild and Magic and probably very, very dangerous. Especially when he was mad.

"Well I'm sorry I asked, I'm sure! How was I to know? I'm just a stupid human, after all," she said, her fear welling up in the form of false bravado. "And I *wish* you'd stop calling me 'human' like that. It makes me sound like an insect or a disease or something. I have a name you know. It's Frankie Maxwell. And who are *you*, anyway? Where am I and how did I get here?"

The unicorn scampered back several steps, as if propelled backward by the force of her words. He stopped and looked at her intently, with huge eyes that were bright blue one minute, bright green the next. He slowly walked back again.

"You really do not know where you are?"

"How would I know?" Frankie retorted, taking a few steps toward him. "If I knew where I was, I wouldn't ask. All I know is, I fell through the big portrait on the wall at my Granddad's house into some cold, white slimy stuff, and ended up here, lying face down on the floor! You didn't see a necklace come flying this way, did you?" She flicked her gaze around the cabin, but didn't see the necklace. "Anyway," she said to him, "I think I want to go home now—even if you *are* a unicorn. I always thought unicorns were magic and wonderful. But now you've spoiled it. If I want lectures, I can stay home!"

He walked up to her and rubbed his soft nose against her arm. His warm breath smelled of wild flowers. And when he touched her, her mind filled with soft visions of fairies and nymphs and wide open meadows filled with flowers stretching toward the sun.

"I did not intend to lecture you, human, er, . . Frankie. I become a bit peevish when I have to convince someone that I exist. You probably would, too." He bent his front right leg and bowed low until his horn nearly touched the ground. Then he straightened up and looked at her.

"My name is Aldebaran, and I welcome you to Terra. You can go home any time you wish," he said. "Just hold that pink stone you brought with you, walk into that portrait on the wall, and you will be back where—*and when*—you started. The pink stone, you see, is made of rose quartz. It vibrates with the energy of pure love. It is the *key* to the door between the worlds. It is the key to Everything, actually."

Frankie felt a shiver run up her spine, and the hair on the back of her neck prickled up. She had found it—the door between the worlds—just as her Aunt Cassie had! But she had forgotten all about the pink heart-shaped stone. She had picked it up from the floor right after she landed and her hand was clenched so hard around it that her fingers were white and numb.

"But I hope you will not leave just yet," Aldebaran continued, his voice getting soft and rumbling, "we would like to get to know you. Not many people find their way between worlds—and never without a very good reason. There might just be something important for you here."

Frankie flushed with guilt as she suddenly remembered all of her big talk about coming to this world to save Aunt Cassie. If this really was the place Aunt Cassie had talked about, then this was where Frankie needed to be to help her, to find that lost part of her! But Frankie was confused. Part of her wanted to stay and do what she could to save Aunt Cassie, and have her own great adventure. But another part of her wanted to plunge back into the portrait and go home while she still had the chance. What if she couldn't help Aunt Cassie? And what if she really couldn't get back home? It was one thing to wish for an adventure in the warm comfort of her grandparents' dining room, where an adventure was unlikely to happen, and quite another thing to suddenly find herself smack in the middle of one. Had wishing made it so? Frankie wasn't feeling quite so brave anymore.

And what about her Dad? He would be *furious* when he found out she was gone. How long had she been here? No one would ever think to look for her in the portrait, of all places. Well, maybe Aunt Cassie would. When the family realized she was gone, would Aunt Cassie figure out where she had gone and tell them? Or would the door between the worlds have to remain a secret? They probably wouldn't believe her, anyway. Would Aunt Cassie come after her, herself, even though she was too weak to do it? Or would her Dad come here to get her? That would *really* be a nightmare!

Frankie shook her head. All these thoughts swirling around in her head were making her dizzy. She walked past the unicorn and out the doorway and stood on the grass, staring off into the thick woods and the bright blue sky as she tried to take it all in.

"Well, what are you going to do?" the unicorn demanded. He seemed to be getting a bit agitated, prancing back and forth from hoof to hoof. "We cannot wait here all day. We should travel while it is still light. . . marauders in the dark, you know. Do not worry that your father will find you gone. You can stay as long as you like and still get back home by the time you left. . ."

Unicorns might be Magic, Frankie thought, but they certainly didn't make much sense. She wished he would just be quiet for a minute and stop confusing her.

"Aldebaran," a voice broke in, "I don't think you're doing a very good job of it."

Frankie looked up in surprise to see a girl about her own age walking toward them.

"She's probably tired and hungry and very, very confused. And maybe just possibly a little bit afraid," the girl said, and the unicorn turned slightly pink around the edges. "Let's take her home, where she can rest and eat and sort it all out. Uriel will know what to do."

At last, Frankie thought, someone who understands. The girl was very pretty, but in a different-than-usual sort of way. She was about five feet tall, with thick dark hair down to her waist. She wore sandals on her feet and a simple tunic that came down to her knees. The tunic was a dusty pink. . . no, it was blue. . . no, purple. As Frankie watched, the tunic actually changed colors and shimmered, and the color seemed to spread out into the air around her, like when you color over the lines with crayons. This was as bad as the unicorn changing sizes and fading in and out!

"Everything around here shimmers and changes entirely too much," Frankie said peevishly, stomping her foot.

The other girl laughed a light tinkly laugh, and her tunic turned warm and yellow like the wild flowers blooming furiously around the cottage.

"You're just not used to it yet." She held out her hands and Frankie took them in her own. "My name is Ilayna, and I'm so glad you came."

Frankie liked her immediately. "But where am I? What *is* this place?"

"Why you're on Terra, in the mountains between the city of Alaris and the fortress Kelghard," Ilayna said. "We're going home to Alaris. Will you come and visit with us for a time?"

"Well I'd like to," Frankie said, shuffling her feet a little in the dirt, "but I've probably been gone too long already. You don't know my Dad. . . he'll be really mad." She thought a minute, retrieved an idea she'd had on more than one occasion before, then grinned and added, "of course, he's already mad at me anyway, so what difference will it make?"

"But he will not even know you are gone," Ilayna said.

"That is exactly what I told you," added the unicorn with a snort. "Time is different here, Frankie. When you travel between the worlds you pass through space *and* time. No matter how long you stay here, when you go back home, you will arrive just when you left."

"But that's impossible," Frankie said.

"So are unicorns," Aldebaran answered with a snort.

Frankie knew he had her there. Aunt Cassie had said something about time being different. Of course, Frankie hadn't really believed it. But she figured that believing in this time thing was no weirder than believing in unicorns or in traveling to other worlds through a portrait. And it really *would* explain how Aunt Cassie could say she had been here for years when she wasn't really missing from home for any time at all.

"Do come home with us for a visit, Frankie," Ilayna said, clapping her hands. "Uriel would love to meet you and we will have such fun together."

How could she refuse, especially if her Dad would never know? It was like getting a free pass. Frankie went back into the cottage to look for her aunt's necklace. It was lying on the floor near where she had landed. She slipped the chain around her neck, carefully tucking the medallion under her tee shirt for safe-keeping. Then she slipped the pink heart-shaped key stone into the pocket of her jeans and went outside to see what kind of world she had landed in.

ఞ 4 ఞ

A Parallel World

"**H**ome" was in the valley at the foot of the mountain, and it looked a long way off. Frankie was not much of a hiker and didn't really like anything in the way of strenuous exercise. She was more interested in mental things than physical things. Hadn't she just gotten a *D* in gym class? She'd far rather curl up in the big green wing chair in the television room at home and read a book or allow her wild curiosity to roam around the internet than do anything that might make her tired and sweaty. But here she was, heading out on a hiking trip!

Fortunately, the sky was clear and blue, the weather was balmy, and it was fast, easy going, even for her. Aldebaran said he thought the gravity here was lighter than on Earth, which made the hiking easier. Frankie was sure that the company and all the new sights and sounds helped, too. They walked for an hour or so, with the girls laughing and teasing the unicorn who, to their fiendish delight, turned slightly pink now and then from the attention. But he took it without grumbling and nudged them along if they started to fall behind. They followed a wide dirt road straight ahead, down into the valley toward the opposite mountain, which soared up into the clouds.

"There it is, Frankie!" Ilayna pointed as they rounded a sharp curve by a grove of ancient oak trees, "Look! There's Alaris."

Frankie stopped in mid-step, her mouth hanging open in awe and surprise as she caught her first glimpse of the city, tucked neatly into the valley below them, between the mountain directly across and the sea down to the left. From Frankie's vantage point, the city was more beautiful than anything she could have imagined.

Boats with brightly colored sails bobbed on the sea at the end of the valley. Tall sparkling buildings rose up in the middle of the valley, surrounded by hundreds of low pastel-colored buildings, all the colors of the rainbow, connected across the city by wide, tree-lined streets. As they continued walking, the road descended into the city in a series of wide terraced steps.

Except for several very tall buildings at the city center, most of the buildings were one or two stories, and the architecture was like nothing Frankie had ever seen. The buildings had simple, straight lines without ornamentation. Many sparkled as if the stone itself contained bits of gold and silver. Some of the buildings had cascading fountains and great angular sculptures. Some of them had wide rooms and verandahs with columns, but no walls, and Frankie could see bits of gauzy curtains framing the openings or billowing out on the breeze. The buildings seemed to absorb the sun's light and hold it just under the surface to create a pulsing glow.

"The stone they use to construct the buildings," Ilayna told her when she asked about it, "absorbs the sunlight. At night, the buildings glow with the light they have stored during the day. Is it not the same where you come from?"

Frankie said she'd never seen anything like it and told Ilayna about the brick and concrete and glass buildings at home and how electricity and lamps provided the light.

"The different colors of the buildings are a reflection of the mood and the energies of the people inside them," Aldebaran added. "If enough people in one building focus on the same feeling or emotion, they can actually change the color of the building because of the way the stone responds to energy. The cloth the people of Alaris use for clothing has the same properties," he said, "it conducts and absorbs energy, and then reflects it back."

Frankie glanced at Ilayna and saw that her tunic was now uniformly bluish purple. She wondered why they didn't have things like that at home. She didn't really understand how it worked, but she loved the effect. There was something warm and welcoming about Alaris, and Frankie didn't know if it was the glowing buildings, the spacious lawns and gardens, the people, or a combination of all of those things that gave that impression. Everywhere Frankie looked there were people, talking and laughing and enjoying themselves, wearing outfits similar to Ilayna's: simple loose-fitting tunics and trousers, in all the rainbow of colors. And as she watched, the colors would pulse out into the air or change before her very eyes.

Frankie lived in Washington, DC, and what she noticed most of all in Alaris was that there were no cars, no trucks, no traffic lights, and no traffic jams. Occasionally Frankie saw small, silent, bullet-shaped objects moving serenely through space about ten feet above the ground, but even when she saw the drivers' faces through the clear windscreens, Frankie couldn't quite consider them to be remotely like cars.

In the very center of the city they came to a park with what looked to Frankie like a giant ice sculpture in the center. Aldebaran told her it was clear quartz crystal, and it stood at least fifteen feet high, with one giant ice-clear spike reaching up toward the clouds. It was shaped sort of like the Washington Monument, Frankie thought. At its base were five or six other spikes, each taller than Frankie, but none quite so high as the one in the center. Each of the spikes had six sides.

The giant crystal in the center was mounted on a wide round platform, and it was the focus of plenty of activity. Several people "parked" their vehicles nearby, dropping down lightly to rest on the grass before raising the windscreen section to exit. Each of them brought out a large square object, almost like the battery in Frankie's Dad's car, and deposited the object on the platform at the base of the crystal. The drivers would then wander away toward the other buildings or stop to chat with other people nearby. Frankie and her friends stood and watched this strange procession for several minutes, until there were eight or ten of the silver-colored vehicles lined up in a row and a crowd of people standing around chatting.

Finally someone reversed the procedure—a young man with dark hair, dressed like the other men in tunic and leggings, said good-bye to his friends, walked back to the crystal and retrieved one of the square objects. Then he walked to one of the vehicles and got in. The vehicle smoothly lifted up about ten feet off the ground and flowed silently away from the center of town toward the mountains across the valley.

"What are those things," Frankie asked, "and what were those people doing?"

"Those are air riders," Ilayna told her as they walked away from the crystal park. "They ride the air currents. They are mostly used when people are traveling long distances, from city to city. They are propelled by energy supplied by the giant crystals and stored in those square boxes. Periodically, the owners have to come back to the crystals to recharge the battery."

"You mean they just let it sit next to that crystal for awhile, and it's all charged up and ready to go?" Frankie asked.

"Why, yes. Don't you have anything like that where you live?"

"Well, not really," Frankie answered, knowing she was getting in a little over her head. "We have cars and trucks — millions of them, everywhere — but they run on gasoline. They have to stop at a gas station once in awhile to fill up the tank and they have to pay each time. It's very expensive. My Dad says the cost of gas is outrageous — like highway robbery. We have some electric cars, but I'm not sure how they work."

"Well, that sounds like this, except we don't have to pay anything," Ilayna said.

But Frankie wasn't so sure.

"Do the crystals supply all the power you use?" she asked.

"They supply much of it," Aldebaran told her. "But they are also able to use wind power and the power of the tides."

Frankie thought those were pretty good ideas, far better than being dependent on oil.

As they crossed the center of the city and headed toward Ilayna's home in the lower part of the valley, she pointed out the different buildings and told Frankie a little about the city and the people who lived there. The Exchange Center, where people brought their goods to exchange in trade for other goods and services, glowed sparkling deep green. The color, according to Aldebaran, was one of balance, wisdom, and harmony.

Farther on, they passed the Science Center, with its gleaming blue laboratories, observatories, and libraries; the red glowing Energy Center; the orange and yellow Performing Arts Center with its blue cultural wing; and the green-blue Aquatic Center down by the shore.

Not far past the Aquatic Center, they came to Ilayna's home. Ilayna told her that the children in Alaris leave home at age 10 or 12 to study. Usually by that age they have some idea of their interests, and they study a subject with a teacher until they want to move on and study something else. Ilayna lived with Uriel, a Healer. Ilayna was her apprentice and had been living with Uriel for three years, learning all about herbs, energy, and crystals. Frankie thought that sounded a thousand times more interesting than studying history and arithmetic!

♥   ♥   ♥

An old woman and a huge cat were waiting for them on the wide front porch when they reached the house, and the woman greeted all three of them with warm hugs. The big orange cat rubbed up against Ilayna's legs, playfully batted Aldebaran's tail with an orange and white paw, and then positioned himself at a distance to watch Frankie until he made up his mind about her.

"Don't mind Sebastian," the woman said, "he's just playing hard-to-get. He'll be sitting in your lap telling you all about how we abuse him in no time. Come up on the porch and let's have a look at you."

They called it a porch, but it looked more like a Roman temple or something to Frankie, with a wide smooth stone floor, and a roof held up by columns in the corners. There were no walls, and the curtains drawn up on each side of the columns billowed out with the warm salty breeze from the sea, which was no more than two city blocks away. There wasn't much furniture, just a couple of small tables and a few chairs set out to face the water. The porch led off to a long low building, with three sections of different colors.

"Why is the house three different colors?" Frankie asked Ilayna, pointing out each one. She felt too shy to ask anything of the imposing old woman, who was not like any old woman she had ever seen.

But the woman answered her, anyway. "Because each section is different. That blue section is the library, the middle white section is my laboratory where I keep my herbs and crystals, and the pink section at the back has our living quarters," Uriel explained.

She told Frankie that the building materials used here were like those used in the city, and they pick up the energy around them, reflecting its color. "Let me explain it this way: If you fill a white porous bowl with raspberry or grape juice, and you let it sit for a long time, sooner or later the bowl itself will start to turn pink or red. It picks up the color of what is inside. These walls do the same thing, in a way, except they pick up the color and energy of thoughts and emotions rather than the color of a liquid. Do you understand?"

Frankie nodded, even though she was not quite sure that she did. But who was going to argue with this woman? This was no bent and frail old lady, like she had seen at home. This woman looked like she had lived a long, long time and used every one of those years to get taller, stronger, and wiser. To Frankie, she looked like some kind of Goddess. She looked like the Mother of Time.

Uriel stood about six feet tall. Her gleaming white hair hung straight and thick to her waist. Her large, wide-set eyes changed color as Frankie looked at them, almost as much as the unicorn's. So did her hooded floor-length dress, which was a longer version of Ilayna's tunic. As Frankie looked at her, she could almost see images of how Uriel had looked at different times in her life. Her image seemed to flicker in a subtle way, just like Aldebaran's did from time to time. Frankie wasn't exactly sure if she was really seeing either of them as they really were, and wondered if she was merely seeing an image being held in place for her, an image that wobbled and shifted from time to time as if from some sort of interference, like a television image flickers during a storm.

"Come with me, dear," Uriel said, taking Frankie's hand and leading her toward the main building at the back of the big, wide porch. "You must be tired. I was looking in my master crystal and saw you coming, so I have brewed some herb tea and made some orange cake for a snack.

"Ilayna, you just relax here while I help Frankie find something more comfortable to wear and get the tea things. And you, Aldebaran," she turned and actually winked at the unicorn, "I think I may even have a little treat for you, too."

Frankie followed Uriel into the house. They passed through the library and the laboratory before crossing another porch that led to the living quarters. Everything was neat, well organized, streamlined, and modern. And Frankie could feel a difference in the atmosphere of each section of the house as they passed through. She wondered if she was actually feeling the difference in the energies. The laboratory felt cool and crisp, almost stimulating. Shelves filled with hundreds of jars of herbs lined the walls, and beautiful colored stones of all sizes and shapes covered almost every available surface. Some of the stones looked like the ones she had seen on the portrait frame in her aunt's room. Before she had time to ask about them, though, they moved into the residence wing and Uriel showed her into a bedroom with a closet full of tunics and sandals.

"These were left by previous students, Frankie, and I'm sure you'll find one that you feel comfortable in." Uriel told her before she left. "You can freshen up just across the hall. I'll be fixing tea in the kitchen. Join the others on the porch when you're ready. But don't feel that you have to rush."

The closet was lined with the beautiful purple stones Frankie had seen throughout the house. She wondered what they were for as she chose a long tunic, like the one Uriel wore. Ilayna told her later that the purple stones are amethysts, and they clean and transform energy. The stones were put in the closet to sort of "dry clean" the energy that was soaked up during the day by the special fabrics. Frankie was beginning to realize that this kind of personal energy was very important in Alaris, and she wondered if people at home had energy like this.

Frankie folded her jeans, sweater, and tee shirt and put them in a neat pile on the bed. Then she strapped on a pair of sandals and put on the tunic. It hung straight from her shoulders and swished softly about her feet as she walked. The material was softer than any fabric she had ever seen, even satin or velvet. And it shimmered and glowed as it moved around her. She was glad to find that the dress had pockets, because she wanted to keep the pink heart-shaped key stone close at hand. She popped it into a pocket and went out to join the others.

"You look beautiful!" Ilayna said as Frankie joined them and settled into a rocking chair on the porch, carefully tucking the folds of the dress around her legs. The sun was just setting over the lower valley and the water, and bright reds and pinks, oranges and purples all blazed across the horizon.

Ilayna gave a little sigh as she watched it, too. Even Aldebaran, who was settled down on some large cushions not far from Frankie's chair, made some contented little snorty, whiffling noises through his nose. Frankie wondered if that was the sound of a happy unicorn, and grinned at the very idea of it.

As they sat together watching the sunset, the unicorn tried to explain how this could be a totally separate world from her own, separated only by a simple portrait at her grandfather's house.

"Terra is a parallel world to Earth," Aldebaran told her. "There are many parallel worlds that were 'split off' at times of great stress on Earth, when there was great upheaval caused by man or Nature. Each time that happens, the original

Earth continues on its course, and a split-off world moves off by itself into its own future—a future with a different choice or outcome. The war is averted or the earthquake is not so destructive. But all of the split-off worlds remain connected by doorways or portals that span the distance of time and space."

Even though Frankie was not sure she understood it all, she was happy to sit in the twilight listening to a unicorn talk of magic worlds that refused to be destroyed.

"This world is Terra, and it split off from Earth centuries ago," Aldebaran said, "centuries before history was even recorded on Earth, when the city of Atlantis was the center of civilization."

Frankie thought she had heard of Atlantis, but she thought it was a mythical place that never really existed. She mentioned this to the unicorn, who snorted in disgust. She was getting used to hearing that particular snort.

"Yes, well, humans in your world often do not believe in anything they cannot prove. The crisis for Atlantis," he explained, "was one of technology over humanity. The people of Atlantis discovered the giant crystal you saw in the city of Alaris and they learned how to use the energy in crystals and other stones. A wealth of science and technology grew up around the giant crystal that made life easier for everyone, very much like the technology in your world today."

The unicorn readjusted his legs under himself and paused for a moment before continuing.

"Unfortunately," he said, "when a group of scientists and political leaders tried to use the giant crystal as a weapon to conquer other parts of the world, they overloaded the systems and blew themselves up. They destroyed all of Atlantis and most of the rest of the world in the process."

Frankie stared down at her hands guiltily, as if she were somehow responsible for what happened.

"So *this* world split off just before that explosion,"

Aldebaran continued, "And in *this world*, those leaders were overthrown before they could do much damage, and the people learned other ways to use their technology. Oh, they still made war, as humans tend to do, but they did not destroy themselves."

Uriel came back out onto the porch with a tray loaded down with orange cakes, tea, mugs, and plates. She served the girls, then gave Aldebaran a plate with some cakes that looked like English muffins.

"Your favorite oat cakes, my dear," she told him, patting his head just behind the golden horn. Frankie didn't know much about magical creatures, but she couldn't imagine anyone in any world who could get away with touching anywhere near that magical horn — without permission, anyway. It only increased Frankie's respect for the imposing old woman.

Uriel put the tray on a small table and pulled her own chair into the circle with the others. The chair was made of heavy dark wood with a high back carved all over with stars and moons and magical symbols.

"Oh yes, we have had our share of wars, Frankie," she said as she helped herself to some tea. "It seems that having wars is part of the human condition, a stage of development that all humans must work through. Some do it faster than others." Then she turned to Aldebaran. "I take it you have not told her of recent events?"

"No, Uriel," Aldebaran answered, "I thought I would save that for another time. I think Frankie has had sufficient new things to absorb in one day."

"But she needs to know about the raiding parties, Aldebaran," Uriel said. "I have a feeling. . . it is better if she is warned."

Frankie shivered suddenly, even though the evening was still warm. She noticed that the magnificent sunset had finally ended, and the world outside the softly glowing columns of the porch was dark. It suddenly occurred to her that there might be something menacing out there, watching them. And if Uriel was concerned about it, it must be pretty bad.

"What do you mean, raiding parties?" Frankie asked. "Do they come *here?*"

"Not often, dear," Uriel said, "but you should be aware of them. They're a group of ruffians from Kelghard, a not very civilized place on the other side of the mountain. Now and then, they come to Alaris and steal our books and our crystals. They know that we have ways of using energy to improve our environment, but they don't know how to do it. They just think that sooner or later they'll steal the right magic wand, or something, and then they will be able to do it, too." She paused a moment, sipping her tea and staring out into the twilight.

"We taught them how to use these powers once, a few hundred years ago," she said quietly, as if she didn't quite want to say the words out loud, "but they started to use them for conquest and terror. They did not want peace, they wanted to rule over everyone else, just like those who destroyed your Atlantis. So we stopped teaching them, because we did not want them to turn the power against us or to destroy things that could not be repaired. Fortunately, those who had the knowledge died without passing the secrets along. But that has not stopped them, because they know that we have knowledge and power that they do not have—and they want it badly."

"And now they want very much to know where the doors are to the other worlds—or at least where one door is," the unicorn added. "Their leader, Janra, fancies herself quite a warrior, and I have heard on the wind that she readies herself to conquer—first Alaris and then *your* world—and any other world she can find her way into."

"She can't do that! *Can* she?" Frankie started up in outrage, dropping her heavy stoneware mug so that it shattered on the glowing stone floor. Horrified at what she'd done, she apologized profusely as she knelt down to pick up the pieces, placing them gently on the table.

"It *is* possible," Aldebaran said. "It has happened before. Kelghard was founded centuries ago by invaders from your world. It is possible that they will someday find a way back."

"Well, why don't you go and fight them, and show them that they can't get away with this stuff? Use the giant crystal and show them who's boss," Frankie said.

"How fierce you are, Frankie!" Aldebaran said.

"Well, I, ah. . . no, not really" Frankie said, remembering her own embarrassing run-ins with bullies at school. She didn't like wars, but she really hated the idea of ruthless raiders destroying Alaris and hurting her friends. "But can't you stop them from raiding Alaris? You know, have the police put them in jail or something?"

"We have our own ways of dealing with them, Frankie," Uriel said. "We *can* fight that way, but we don't like to do it. We have learned that violence only begets violence. Responding to their actions in kind merely continues the cycle. But there is another important reason: We Alarans are empathic people—we physically feel other people's pain. The energies generated by violence and war are hardly tolerable to us. So we try to deal with them in other ways."

"And the point here is not whether the Alarans fight back or not," Aldebaran said, "the point is that we must caution you: Janra is greedy and looking for conquest, here and in your world. And she has spies everywhere to help her gather information. If you are to stay any length of time with us, Frankie, do not tell anyone where you came from or how you got here."

"And whatever you do," Uriel told her, "do not let anyone know about that stone."

"What stone, old woman?"

The voice was unexpected and harsh, and this time Uriel almost dropped *her* mug in surprise. The man who stood on the edge of the porch was tall, well muscled, and definitely savage looking. He wore something like buckskin trousers, and there was an archer's bow and a quill filled with feathered arrows over his shoulder. He reminded Frankie very much of the warriors in her dream. Or the bad guys in the stories about Robin Hood or the Crusades. He held a very large knife pointed at Uriel's throat.

Frankie trembled in her chair, afraid to move. Aldebaran suddenly grew very big and fierce, like the unicorn in her dream, and then he blurred, faded, and completely disappeared right before her eyes.

Uriel regained her composure and seemed to grow in height and strength. She sat bolt upright, unflinching, and looked straight into her attacker's eyes. Her tunic slowly turned from light lilac to a dark, reddish purple, and Frankie could almost see waves of energy radiating out all around her. Thunder sounded in the air and lightning crackled across the sky. A group of men came out of the shadows behind the warrior, as if pulled into the circle of light against their will. They made funny protective motions with their hands and muttered under their breath.

"I do not remember inviting you to our party, Malus," Uriel said with a voice flat and cold like ice, "but I have no quarrel with you and, since you are here, you are welcome to some refreshment. Would you care for some cakes or tea?"

"I want none of your witch brews, old woman," he told her. "I have a feeling I would have learned more if I had arrived here sooner. But as it is, I learned that there is a stone to be hidden—and my mistress Janra is always interested in anything that your people try to hide. Where is it? Who has it?"

Uriel reached into her sleeve with a great show of reluctance and brought out a round black stone and held it out to him. "Here is your stone, Malus. Take it and go."

"I don't think so," he said, brushing a heavy lock of dark, dirty hair out of his face. He held the stone up close to a burning torch to inspect it. "If it is so important, you would not give it up so easily. Would you care to try again?"

Where is Aldebaran? Frankie thought frantically. He had vanished completely. If he really was a magic creature, surely he could do something to help them, she thought. She was glad at least that Uriel had suggested that she change her clothes—in her long tunic, which was now the color of pond scum, she didn't look so obviously different from the others. At home, the outfit she'd arrived in made her fit in with the crowd at school. Here, her blue jeans, sweater, and sneakers would have been a dead giveaway!

"Take it," Uriel said, her deep voice like ice, "why would I hide it from you? There is nothing to hide and even if there were, Malus, you are far too perceptive to be deceived. Take it and leave us alone."

"You won't cooperate? Well, fortunately I brought some friends with me who can help me look."

Malus cocked his head toward the men behind him and they swarmed up onto the porch.

Where is Aldebaran? Frankie wondered frantically. How could he just leave them to the mercy of these barbarians?

"Search the women," Malus told his men, "and then search the house. Take anything that looks interesting."

Frankie held tightly to the stone in her pocket. She wanted to hide it, but where? She was too scared to think, and she watched in horror as a tall warrior searched Ilayna, ripping her tunic as he pulled something from her pocket. Frankie could not think of anything to do and, even if she could think of something, she felt too terrified to move. So she sat, and waited to see what would happen next, hoping she could somehow manage to hold onto the pink stone. And again the question leapt across her mind: *Where is Aldebaran?*

She was not able to hold onto it for very long. Malus, himself, was the one who felt the lump in her pocket and reached in to claim the stone. She was too scared to say anything, which was probably good. He didn't take any special notice of it and just dropped it into a bag with the other things they had taken from Ilayna and Uriel.

He reached for the chain around her neck, the one that held Aunt Cassie's medallion, and Frankie was afraid she would scream. She couldn't bear to lose her aunt's necklace. It was bad enough that he took the heart-shaped key stone, but she just could not let him have the necklace, too. She could feel a familiar rise of anger and resentment, and she knew she was going to have to stand up to him, even as she knew that was not a particularly smart thing to do. She was about to jerk her arm away when he saved her the trouble.

He turned away at the sound of a loud crash, followed by several smaller ones. Frankie suddenly envisioned those shelves of bottles of herbs and those hundreds of crystals smashing to the floor. There was yelling in the laboratory, and Frankie heard Uriel's voice raised up like a terrible thunder. Malus held the necklace so tight around Frankie's neck that it was cutting off the circulation, and she was starting to feel very dizzy and light-headed. Finally he let go of the chain and went to see about the trouble, but it was too late for Frankie.

One thought swam through her mind as she started to pass out: *WHERE IS ALDEBARAN?*

The Tapestry of Life

"**B**ut where *were* you?" Frankie wailed at the unicorn. Her hands were so tightly clenched at her sides that the fingernails were cutting into her palms. "Why didn't you stop them? Why didn't you help us? How could you just leave us like that?"

She felt the rage and disappointment well up in her until it was all she could do to keep from raising her clenched fists and pounding them into the unicorn's soft white side. As she stared miserably at him, with tears flowing openly down her face, he walked up right next to her and gently licked them away.

Aldebaran had reappeared the next afternoon as the three women were cleaning up the mess left by Malus and his men. Frankie was taking a breather out on the porch when the unicorn shimmered into form with a flash of sunlight, a glint of gold, and an uproar of dust. Instead of pounding at him, though, Frankie flung her arms around his neck and buried her face in his silky mane.

"Where did you *go*, Aldebaran?"

The unicorn let her cling to him for a moment, then gently eased himself out of her embrace and turned to face her, clearing his throat in a ragged sort of unicorn way.

"I was here the whole time, child," he told her, "but you could not see me."

He followed her into the lab, where the three women had been working. Ilayna and Uriel were putting the last of the crystals back up on the table at the far end of the room and they greeted the unicorn as if nothing unusual had happened. Then they discreetly left the room to take a break of their own and let Frankie and Aldebaran talk alone.

Frankie halted by the herb shelves and stooped to pick up some large pieces of broken glass that had been missed and tossed them into a pile of debris. She was afraid that if she looked at him, she would burst into tears again. His apparent desertion had left her feeling lost and alone, and she was still hurt and angry.

"Malus and his men have such angry *disbelief* in anything truly Magical," he explained, "that even your belief in me — and Uriel's and Ilayna's — could not keep me materialized. It was too painful, even for a unicorn. I was here, though. I saw it all. I saw them knocking over Uriel's jars of herbs and Ilayna's sculptures. I saw them breaking things and picking up things and putting them in their brown sacks to carry back to Janra. I saw Malus reach into your pocket. I wept when he took your key stone. But I could not do anything to help. I am not permitted to interfere."

"Why not?" Frankie asked, kicking her foot out restlessly, and spreading out a mass of broken glass, spilled herbs, and pieces of broken shelving that she had swept into a pile not 10 minutes ago. This was not the answer she wanted to hear.

"You have to remember I am a unicorn," he continued. "I am not a human, not an Alaran, not a warrior. I cannot interfere in the lives of humans except in extreme situations, and even then only in a limited way. There is free will. There are patterns that must play out. Things usually happen for a reason, even if you do not understand what the reason is at the time. I cannot interfere with the unfolding of Life."

But Frankie did not really want to understand what he was trying to tell her. She wanted to believe that he was there to protect her and keep her safe. Of what use was a magical beast, if he wouldn't protect her and vanquish her enemies? All the stories she had read as a child told of magical beasts and men who came to the rescue when needed. Here she'd actually found a magical beast, and he had disappeared just when she needed him! To Frankie, it was a horrible disappointment.

"You see, Frankie," he continued as she busied herself with moving the pile of debris from the floor to the trash can, "there are many of us who watch the progress of the Universe — seraphim, angels, centaurs, dragons, winged lions — you have heard about some of us in myths and legends and great books. Some of us you have not heard about at all and cannot even imagine. And for some of us, the stories went wrong along the way and got all mixed up. You can see some of us if you believe enough and we *want* you to see us, but some of us you cannot see for anything — and some, you probably would not want to."

He shivered a little and his coat turned flat pale gray, as if some of those beings really were too terrible for even a unicorn to see.

"It is not easy to stand and watch, to see things and not do anything, to watch and not intervene. Sometimes it breaks my heart. But it is what I must do. There will be times in your life when you must do that — when you can only stand by and be the witness — and you will know how it feels."

Frankie knew exactly how that felt, for she had only been able to stand by and witness as her mother had died of cancer.

There was nothing that she, or anyone, could do to stop it. It wasn't a role that she ever wanted to have to play again.

"But do you have to be just a witness *now*?" she asked, as she finished cleaning up the pile again and set the dustpan and brush down on a counter. "This can't be right! I didn't exactly expect to get mugged here, you know. I thought Alaris was much nicer, and safer, than home. But it's not, it's just the same. I might as well just go home, now, but I don't know how. Maybe I can't go home now, because they took the key. Will you get the key stone back for me, so I can go home?"

The unicorn slowly shook his head. "I cannot get the key for you. Only you can do that." He looked at her sadly, as if he knew exactly how she felt and he wanted to make it better, but he couldn't. "I might be able to help a little, Frankie, but you have to do it for yourself."

"But how can *I* get it? I'm just a kid. Why *can't* you get it for me?" Her voice screeched out at him as she picked up a piece of a broken shelf and sent it hurtling out of the room.

"My dear," he told her, nudging her arm gently with his nose, "it is *always* up to you—do you not know that? Do they not teach you this where you come from? It is a fundamental rule of Life. You cannot live your life waiting for someone else to come and fix it for you. If you want a change, you must take action yourself. You have to decide what you want, set your intention, and then take action, always taking responsibility for what you do. Whatever you decide you want, you must *believe* it is yours and respond as Life leads you to it. There is a saying you humans have: 'Seeing is believing.' That is actually backwards. You must believe first. If you do not believe, you will not see the opportunity when it presents itself. That is how you work with Life. And when things appear to go *wrong*, it is not so much what happens to you that is important, as how you *respond* to what happens to you. Would you rather sit back safely and act the victim?

"Remember: You *always* have a choice, even if you must choose among options that you do not like, and even if you do not like the things you might have to do once you make the choice—such as what it might take to get the key stone back in order to go home."

Frankie realized the truth of this statement—sometimes she did have to choose between two things when neither of them seemed very good. And sometimes following her choice and facing the consequences was not easy. She wasn't sure what he meant about working with Life or about expecting to get what she wanted, because it seemed that quite often she got the opposite.

The unicorn nudged her to get her full attention and continued. "You know we all will help you as much as we can, no matter what you decide to do. But we cannot decide for you, and we cannot do it for you. You are the only one who can decide what you will do in your life; it is always your choice, and yours alone. And it is your path to travel once you choose it. Sometimes you will be able to take action and sometimes you will only be able to witness or choose how to respond. Sometimes you will be lucky enough to find fellow travelers along the way, but mostly you must travel your path alone—that is just part of being human."

Even though something deep inside told her he was right, Frankie didn't like his answer very much. But she did forgive him.

When they finished cleaning up the house, Aldebaran blinked out of sight again, this time to go elsewhere to do other things, and Frankie wandered outside to think about her dilemma. She found an ancient weeping willow tree by a pond not too far from the house, and she sat down on the grass, with her back against its gnarled trunk. Its sweeping branches formed a green cocoon, and she felt like she was hiding from the world.

She tried to think about what to do, but she felt completely overwhelmed and unprepared. She wondered whether she should even try to get the key stone back, to try to go home. Images of her life at home flashed before her eyes: her mother saying something funny, her father laughing, Frankie and Sam playing out in the yard. That life would be worth going home to. But she didn't have that life anymore, not since her mother had died. And she wasn't sure she wanted to rush back to what was there now. For once in her life, she had the opportunity to sit "outside" and look at her life, and she didn't like what she saw or who she was becoming. She was always trying to be something she wasn't, trying to please everyone, and never quite managing to please anyone, least of all herself. And she didn't think she was the only one. It just seemed that everyone at home was stressed out and unhappy.

It was different here in Alaris. Except for those nasty raiders, the people here seemed very different from the people at home. Uriel and Ilayna didn't seem to be stressed out, and they seemed to accept her just the way she was. She didn't have to do anything special or follow any rules for them to think she was worthy or likable. They even asked her opinion about things and really listened to her when she said something. It might be nice to stay here, she thought, and that way she wouldn't have to worry about finding a way to get the key stone back.

But even if she decided to go back home, she thought, she didn't know how she could do it. How could she ever get the key stone back from Malus and Janra? Maybe Malus had made the decision for her when he took the stone? But no. Aldebaran told her it was her choice to make. But if she chose to go home, getting the key stone back was going to be an almost overwhelming problem.

On top of that, Frankie reminded herself, she still had to figure out how to help Aunt Cassie. Her fingers traced along the chain links on her aunt's pendant and she was thankful that it was still secure around her neck. She remembered *that* was the real reason she was here. That was the important thing. Life in either place—Alaris or home—wouldn't be worth living if she didn't at least try to save Aunt Cassie, now that she was here. It was something she felt she was supposed to do, something she wanted to do more than anything. Even if she didn't know how. And once she did what she had to do, Frankie thought, then she had to be able to get home. Frankie suddenly realized that she couldn't really make a *choice* about going home unless she was actually able to do it. And that brought her right back to the problem of how to get the key stone back.

Except for her mother's death, the problems she had in her life suddenly seemed trivial and stupid to Frankie, compared to the problem of saving Aunt Cassie, getting the key stone back, and getting home. She could see how she had tried so hard to be popular, to be liked by the popular girls and boys at school. She could see how she had worried about being perfect, fitting in, being thin enough or smart enough, or funny enough. And she suddenly wondered, "enough for whom?"

After all, Frankie thought, if she couldn't get back home, what did it matter if she got a *D* in gym? Or if she lost her temper sometimes and dug her heels in and wouldn't back down? If she couldn't get home again, what did it matter if she had put on a bit of weight last year that just didn't seem to want to go away yet? If she never went back to her old school, what did it matter if she wasn't part of the "in" crowd, or if she didn't wear just the right brand of designer jeans?

Frankie remembered that her mother had always said that those wouldn't be the important things that people would remember about her. She'd said they would remember the things that were *really* important: her kindness and her gentleness, her infectious laugh, her intelligence, and how much she loved them. Maybe her mom was right?

She realized suddenly that in learning this, she had already learned something very important from her adventure in Alaris. Maybe those other things weren't really all that important after all, even in her world. Maybe they were only important if she *thought* they were.

♥   ♥   ♥

When she returned to the house, Frankie found Uriel sitting on the porch, working at a wooden tapestry frame. The frame was large and square, with legs attached to two sides and hooking into two slats on the floor, which were connected by a cross piece. It was like a giant square embroidery hoop, and the mid-section of a long length of cloth was caught firmly in its interlocking edges. Uriel no longer looked like the defiant warrior goddess who had confronted Malus. Now, she looked homey and comfortable, just like anyone's loving grand-mother. She was busy working a three-inch-long needle up and down through the stretched material, pulling with it some bright yellow-green thread.

Frankie stood quietly at her shoulder and watched her work. In the tapestry picture, Uriel was filling in the branches of a weeping willow tree in the picture. She had already finished a few red flowers, grass, and a pond in the portion of fabric within the frame. All the fabric to the left of the framed section was already embroidered, and it draped down into a pile on the floor. The fabric on the right was beige and blank, waiting to be embroidered, waiting to come alive as the story unfolded.

As Uriel worked her needle, Frankie picked up the end of the finished fabric and studied the scenes that were already done. She immediately recognized Ilayna and Aldebaran by the cottage in the woods—and there was a figure standing between them, a girl with wavy copper hair, just a bit shorter than Ilayna.

"Why, that's me!" She said, pointing to the figure. It really did look just like her. All of the figures were remarkably accurate.

"Of course, dear," Uriel answered, her needle continuing to move back and forth, in and out.

"And Ilayna is there, and Aldebaran."

Frankie held up the next completed section and watched her whole story in Alaris unfold: There they were, with Frankie just arrived through the cottage-portrait-door; then it showed them walking toward the city, with Frankie running into the field to pick some flowers; then, walking across the main square of Alaris, with its glowing pastel buildings and giant crystal. Here, in the last section, they were sitting on Uriel's porch, and then Malus and his men were storming into the house.

The scene Uriel was working on showed Frankie sitting under the willow tree, trying to decide her future. It was Frankie's whole story, ever since she arrived in this world! And each of the figures was just perfect.

"What comes next?" Frankie whispered, as if she were caught in a spell that she did not want to break: If she stood and watched long enough, maybe Uriel would answer the question for her in the tapestry. But it didn't work.

"I do not know what comes next, my dear," Uriel said, snipping the green thread as she finished the last stitch of the willow's branches, and put down her needle, thread, and scissors. "I cannot continue until you decide what to do, can I? This is *your* story," She cupped Frankie's face in her hand and smiled. "Were you hoping I could tell you what to do?"

Frankie put the beautifully embroidered fabric carefully back in folds on the floor with a heavy sigh. She nodded.

"But I cannot tell you, dear," Uriel said, patting Frankie on the shoulder, "because I do not know. I can only record what has already happened. You are the one who has to make it happen. You are the only one who can create the tapestry, the story of your life."

"I know. Aldebaran told me that—that I have to decide what to do for myself."

"Aldebaran is very wise, dear. You can only benefit from listening to anything he has to say. And have you decided?"

"I think so."

And with that, Frankie sat straight down on the floor, buried her face in her hands, and sobbed.

By the time Uriel came back to the porch with a tray loaded down with hot cranberry nut bread and mugs filled with steaming tea, Frankie had finished crying and was rocking gently in the big armed rocking chair, staring out across the lower valley to the sea. Frankie was learning that food was Uriel's soothing answer to every emergency and she took a mug, a plate, and a napkin from the tray that Uriel offered.

"Feel better now, dear?"

Frankie nodded. She was embarrassed that she had cried in front of Uriel. It just didn't seem very grown up.

"Sometimes a good cry helps tremendously when we've been under a great strain. It lets the emotional energy move. I do it all the time, myself," Uriel said as she put down the tray on a small table between them and sat down. "Do you want to talk about your decision?"

"I'd rather have you tell me what I should do."

"I know, dear, but it is not up to me. It is not even a question of *shoulds*. It is a question of what you *want* to do."

Frankie looked up, surprised. "Is it really? Just a question of what I *want*?"

Uriel nodded, looking surprised herself. "Of course it is. You are the only one who really knows what is best for you to do. You know it deep in your heart, and if you listen very closely you will hear it, or you will feel it, or you will sense it. Your heart *always* knows what is best for you and everyone concerned. . . the hard part is listening and doing what it tells you, especially if your head does not *think* that is what you want. Did your mother not teach you that, dear?"

Frankie nodded. "I think she tried to, but I didn't understand it. I think I'm beginning to, though." She paused for a minute and gazed out at the sea again before she continued, knowing that what she'd just said was true because her heart felt somehow relaxed. "Well, I'm going to get the key stone back, Uriel," she said, putting her mug down on the table with precision. "I think that's what my heart tells me. I don't know how in the world I'm going to get it, but I'm at least going to try. I know it's important. I feel in my heart it's important." She shrugged and looked sheepishly at Uriel, who encouraged her to go on with a nod and a smile.

"It's really weird, though," Frankie continued, "part of me wants to just run away. Another part really wants to just forget the stupid key stone and stay here forever with you and Ilayna and Aldebaran. And then this other part of me feels guilty about wanting to stay instead of trying to get home. And then, of course, I have to save. . . Oh, never mind. I think I'm listening to my heart, but there are so many voices running around in my head I don't know which is which!"

Uriel laughed and poured herself some more tea. "I know dear, sometimes that is the way it is for all of us. Your mind says six different things and your heart says something totally different. You can really feel torn to pieces! But when you listen to your heart, you know what is true—you just may not know *how* you know it. It can be very frustrating and confusing. It is even worse when other people do not believe you or when they want you to do something totally different. Then you hear all their voices, too. But you will *know* if you are following your heart. You will feel it. You will feel calm, and strong, and right, and able to follow it through, even if you know that what you have to do will be difficult."

"But even if my heart says that's what I want to do," Frankie asked, "how will I do it?"

"Oh, you will see, I am certain of it," Uriel said. "When you follow your heart, the Way is always made clear, although sometimes you only see it one step at time. That is how Life works. But really, Frankie, I think you have already seen this happen."

"Me? How?" Frankie asked.

"Why, Life sent you here, did it not? Was there not a desire in your heart, and Life showed you the Way? It is no accident that you fell into our world."

Frankie gasped as she remembered her wishes to have an adventure and to help Aunt Cassie.

"There, you see?" Uriel stood up and sort of dusted her hands together and started to collect the tea things. "All right. If that is your decision, we have much to do. Let me go and get Ilayna so we can make some plans."

"What about Aldebaran?" Frankie asked.

"Do not worry. That unicorn is always around when he is really needed and he can help. That is how unicorns work!" Uriel's voice trailed after her as she left the room. "Of course, the help does not generally come in the way we expect."

In less than an hour they were sitting around the kitchen table: Frankie, Uriel and Ilayna, with Aldebaran standing at one end. They were talking about how Frankie would get into Janra's castle and find the pink heart-shaped key stone.

Frankie didn't have a clue about how she was going to do it—and the very idea scared her to death—but her friends and her heart told her she could do it, *somehow*. When she thought of herself storming the fortress single-handed, she didn't know whether to laugh or to cry. It sounded like the story line for a really bad movie. But the others seemed to take it for granted that she could do it, and they were figuring out how to prepare her. Even their faith in her was scary.

All Frankie could do was sit and listen as they planned it. Ilayna's mother, Janra's sister, might be able to help, they said, but Aradia was watched closely, because Janra didn't really trust her.

"Your mother lives with those creepy warrior people?" Frankie asked, totally shocked. "Who are those guys, anyway?"

"They are descendants of invaders from *your* world," Uriel said. "They came during your Middle Ages, through a door from your world. . ."

"Through the portrait in Aunt Cassie's room?" Frankie was flabbergasted at the idea of an invading army of medieval warriors lining up down the hall of her grandfather's house to go through the portrait to invade Alaris.

"Probably not, Frankie," Aldebaran said. "That portrait probably did not exist then. This was about 900 years ago of your time. And there are many doors between the worlds."

"They settled in Kelghard and built a fortress and a village, recreating the life they had left behind," Uriel said. "There are legends, though, that at one time, a woman warrior from Kelghard tried to conquer Alaris. Legend has it that she studied with the great wise woman, Cybele, and then returned to Kelghard to train an invading army. In the end, though, she was defeated."

"And until recently, they have mostly left Alaris alone," Aldebaran added.

"Yes," Ilayna said, "until my Aunt Janra decided to follow in her ancestor's footsteps and try to conquer Alaris!"

"And your mother lives there with them?" Frankie asked.

"Oh yes," Ilayna answered. "My mother is Janra's sister. They both came here to Alaris when they were about my age to study with Unarius, one of the Wise Ones, and learn the Alaris ways. My mother fell in love with Unarius' son, Aldreth. They were married and I was born."

Frankie could tell from Ilayna's smile that her memories were fond ones. But her face clouded over as she continued. "My father was killed when I was seven, during Janra's first raid of Alaris."

Ilayna's face suddenly took on a lost and pained look, and Frankie suspected that her own face looked much the same when she thought about her mother. Frankie got up and gave Ilayna a hug.

"It's awful, isn't it?" she said. "I do know how you feel. My mother died last year and I still can't quite believe it. I don't want to believe it. It's too horrible to believe."

Ilayna hugged her back and the two girls knew they shared a terrible aching grief.

"My mother moved back to Kelghard to do what she could to keep my Aunt Janra from making more trouble," Ilayna said after wiping away a stray tear and taking a drink of warm tea from the mug that Uriel put on the table in front of her. "But Aunt Janra believes all the old stories of power and conquering. Mother might be able to help us, but if she shows any interest in your key stone," Ilayna told Frankie, "Janra will realize that it is important, and we'll never get it back. And if Aunt Janra catches my mother doing anything to help us, she'll get even somehow. They are both very powerful, but Janra can be more powerful than my mother, because she doesn't hold back out of love or compassion. All she cares about is power and conquest."

"It's really strange that they haven't changed much in all the time they've lived here," Frankie said. "It's like they still live in the Middle Ages. And here they are, close to Alaris, which is like two centuries in the future. You would think they would want to make things better, to live better lives."

"Perhaps it serves them, somehow, to remain as they are," Uriel said, "to keep the people uneducated and poor."

"Well, it certainly serves Aunt Janra, doesn't it," Ilayna added, "because she gets to be Queen of Everything!"

The more Frankie heard, the more afraid she became about confronting this woman. But her friends were not so worried. They told her that Ilayna's grandfather, Unarius, would teach her all kinds of things that would help her in her quest, things that sounded weird and frightening to Frankie, like how to move things with her mind or how to make herself invisible. It sounded impossible, but Frankie understood that the power the Alarans used had to do with using energy. They harnessed and used the energies of crystals. They focused their own personal energies so strongly that their very thoughts could create and become material, solid things. They could "tune in" like a radio receiver to read the thoughts in other people's minds and use their own energy to move physical objects.

These were the ways the people of Alaris "fought" to repel Janra's army. It didn't hurt that the people in Kelghard lived in fear and superstition, just as the people did during Earth's Middle Ages. That's why Malus had called Uriel a witch, and why his men made protective motions with their hands when Uriel's tunic turned colors and she called down the thunder and lightning.

Frankie wanted to believe that she could learn these skills and actually use them to help her get the key stone back and save Aunt Cassie. She really did.

But she wondered how good they would be against swords and arrows and brute strength. In her dream, she had seen two warriors fight. And she wondered—and worried—if the warriors here were that ferocious, or worse.

❧ 6 ❧

The Crystal Master

Frankie's teacher, Unarius, gave her a chime to strike very lightly, and the sound of one clear perfect note seemed to go on forever. It started loud and full and round when she first struck the chime. Then it lost some of its body and thinned out. But it kept going until it finally just seemed to move out of range so that she couldn't hear it anymore except deep inside her head and her bones.

"It's beautiful, isn't it?" Unarius asked her after the last vibrations were gone.

It was more beautiful than anything she had ever heard, that one perfect note. She smiled and mentally pinched herself as she put her head back and looked up at him—all seven feet of him. He had huge piercing violet eyes that seemed to look right down into that part of her that held all the secrets she had ever had or ever would have. And those penetrating eyes were set into a face that was gentle and wise. If ever there was a gentle giant, Frankie thought, Unarius was it. And, like Uriel, he looked as if he had been around when Time began.

"Did you notice how the sound seemed to just fade away slowly as if it was carried away on the wind?" he asked her.

Oh yes, she had noticed all right. It still seemed to be vibrating through her mind, even though she couldn't actually hear it with her ears anymore.

"Everything I will teach you has to do with energy. This is a demonstration of sound waves," he told her. "You must always remember: Just because you cannot see energy does not mean it is not there."

"Do you mean like radio waves and television waves?" Frankie asked. She was not exactly sure how they worked, but she knew they existed—invisibly—and somehow made the sound and picture move from the broadcast station to her radio or television set at home.

It took her teacher a minute or two before he responded. Frankie had not seen any televisions or radios since she had been in Alaris, so maybe he didn't know what she meant. Unarius put one hand flat on the top of her head and got very quiet and still. His eyes sort of rolled back a bit. He seemed to be listening to something she could not hear, straining to hear it. And there was something about him that changed, too, that she couldn't quite put her finger on. Her aunt had done this once or twice, too, but she didn't know what it meant.

To Frankie, it felt like his body was still there, but he was no longer in it—as if the inner part of him had gone off into her head or her world to find out about television and radio and he hadn't come back yet. But Frankie thought that sounded pretty odd, even if that was how it seemed. Suddenly, though, he was "back," all of him right there with her, alert and smiling.

"Yes, my smart one," he said, putting a friendly hand on her shoulder. "Your radio and television waves are a wonderful example. We have similar devices here, but they look different and are called by different names. Now, let us go to my workroom and see what else we can discover about energy."

Ilayna had arranged for her grandfather, Unarius, to teach Frankie the skills she would need in order to get the key stone back from Janra's fortress. Unarius was the Crystal Master of Alaris, and he was the one who taught people to tap into and harness the energies of the giant crystal. On her first visit, he told Frankie that getting the key stone back was a simple matter, once she knew how to use energy. He made it sound so easy.

Every morning Frankie would have breakfast with Uriel and Ilayna, and then she would leave them to their herbal work while she walked across the valley toward the mountain, to the other side of the pond by the weeping willow, to Unarius' house for her lessons.

His house was very much like Uriel's, but instead of neat orderliness, here was comfortable disarray. Where Uriel's laboratory was filled with rows of beautiful crystals and gem stones or neat little bottles all carefully labeled and filled with different kinds of herbs and seeds, the floor of Unarius' workroom was stacked with books and the tables were covered with chimes, lenses, prisms, magnetic marbles, and all kinds of things that worked with energy. In a way, it was like going to a giant toy store every day, and once Frankie got used to Unarius and felt comfortable with him, she really began to look forward to her visits.

"What you have to remember, Frankie," Unarius told her, holding up a big chunk of clear crystal, "is that energy is everywhere and in everything, and it is just waiting for you to come along and use it. It is like one of your lamps that has been turned off: If you do not know where the switch is, or if you do not know it is a lamp, or if you do not believe it can light up at all and do not bother to look for a switch, then you will not have light." Unarius held the crystal briefly to his forehead and it started to glow, from inside. "People who *know* that the lamp can light up and who know where the switch is — how to turn it on and use it — are the ones who get the benefit from it. The others miss out and just do not see the light."

Frankie groaned at the pun and he winked at her. The crystal light blinked off and he set it gently down on the table as he continued.

"So. . . now we have to teach you how to turn that lamp on." He lightly touched the middle of her forehead as he said it, and Frankie felt a strange buzzing vibration run back through her head and up to her crown. As she was pondering this strange sensation, Unarius cleared away some books and arranged a set of three metal interlocking rings on one of the tables. He looked at them for a moment, his brows furrowed in concentration, and then each ring, one at a time, opened and separated from the others.

"How did you do that?" Frankie gasped in surprise.

"Matter," he said, "all the so-called solid things, is made up of atoms, tiny little things all spinning around together in a kind of magnetic attraction dance. But the atoms are so small, and they spin around so very fast, that you cannot see or feel the movement. When I unlocked the rings," he told her, as if this were perfectly normal, "I merely asked the atoms in the rings to dance away from each other."

"Sure!" Frankie said, not quite believing what she'd seen and certainly not believing it could be so easy. He called this talking to the atoms and moving things with his mind *telekinesis*, and that was her first lesson on using energy from the Crystal Master of Alaris.

Unarius continued to astonish her with his demonstrations. He demonstrated using *telepathy* by plucking random thoughts out of her head and repeating them to her: "Really, Frankie, of *course* there is organization here in my humble workshop! You just cannot see it!"

"That must be because I don't believe it!" Frankie laughed.

"Precisely so!" Unarius laughed, too, and then he picked up a large piece of clear crystal, stared into it and described her Thanksgiving morning argument in the kitchen with her father. He said you can see across time and space, to see future and past events, even in other places by *scrying* or looking into a crystal or a bowl of water and using *clairvoyance*—looking and sensing with your mind. And all the time he kept saying that Frankie could do all these things. It was just a question of believing she could do them and learning how. And she kept trying to believe he was right.

Today they were sitting on high stools at the table in his workroom, talking about the energy and vibrations of crystals and gems.

"Stones, gems and colors, like everything else, also have their own unique energy fields," Unarius told her, "and people respond to that energy all the time—when they pick out jewelry or clothing to wear, they are responding to the energies or vibrations of the colors or the gems. Here in Alaris, of course, we let the clothing respond to *our* energies rather than the other way around!"

Unarius picked up a rough piece of pink stone that was sitting on top of a big book on the window sill and tossed it up and down in his hand. Then he handed it to Frankie.

"Do you know what that stone is called?"

"No," she answered, "but it looks like the key stone that Malus took, the one from the frame of the portrait that opened the door to Alaris."

"Right," he said. "It is called rose quartz. Its energy is one of unconditional Love." Unarius grinned at her and picked up a big heavy book with worn leather covers from one of the stacks and blew the dust off. He shoved a collection of prisms out of the way, causing rainbows to dance across the wall as the light hit them, as he opened the book out on the table.

"It is interesting that rose quartz was used as the key to the door between worlds. Obviously, it was selected for a reason, because of its energy qualities. Of course, one must always remember that Love is always the key. It is the key to *everything*. But I wonder if there was another, more specific reason?

"The other stones on the picture frame you described would have been selected for their qualities, as well. Let me see. . ." he consulted the old yellowed book. He kept looking until he found a picture that looked almost exactly like. . .

"That's the picture in Aunt Cassie's room!" Frankie jabbed the picture with her finger as soon as she saw it. "Why is this picture here? What is this book?"

"It is one of the books of the Old Wisdom. It is hard to find this information in book form—usually one must look through the crystals for the information. Janra got her hands on a few of these old books at one point and we are hoping that she does not understand them." He smiled and shrugged his shoulders. "Most people prefer using crystal projections because they hold a clearer image and do not take up as much room. I just happen to like old books."

No kidding, Frankie thought as she looked around the room. The front half of the work room was almost floor-to-ceiling books. Some of them looked like they had been written centuries ago. She wondered if he had read them all. She also wondered what he meant by crystal projections.

"I will teach you all about crystal projections later. You will like those, I think, but right now, let us finish looking up the stones in your picture frame. . ." He ran his finger quickly down the column of old hand-written print. Frankie leaned in to see the picture and try to read, too. But the print was very faded and she couldn't make it out.

"Here it is, just as I thought." Unarius jabbed at the paper with his finger and a tiny piece on the edge broke off and fluttered to the floor. He read the text to himself, muttering and nodding. "Black tourmaline, to protect your side of the door, of course. . . uh, huh, then aventurine, the stone of adventure. . . then fluorite as the middle stone, to provide balance between the two worlds, yes, yes. . . with topaz and rose quartz, to set the spiritual and loving tone for the journey . . . finished off with a tabular double-terminated clear quartz crystal to strengthen the vibrations of the others and provide more balance between the two worlds."

He slammed his palm down on the page, sending up a cloud of dust, and beamed at Frankie. "Very good. Quite a well-designed portal. The person who made it was perceptive and wise. You see?"

She didn't. She had no idea what that last one was, but she did know that it hadn't been in the frame, and she told him so.

"What do you mean? Are you saying that the book is wrong?"

"No, there was a hole for another stone, the shape of a stop sign except it had six sides. . ." she drew the shape in the dust on the table when his face showed he didn't know what she meant. "But there was no stone in it." Frankie closed her eyes and tried to see in her mind the bottom piece of the picture frame, just to be sure. "There was black. . ."

"That is the tourmaline," Unarius said. "It absorbs negative energy and protects against it."

"Then light green. . ."

"The aventurine, holding the adventure and surprise of the portal itself, with a bit of good luck to see you on your way."

"Then there was a funny pyramid one that was bluish purple," Frankie said, following along the line with her mental vision.

"That one is fluorite," Unarius said. "On the other side it is a pyramid, too, like two pyramids stuck together by the bottoms. It provides balance."

"Then light blue. . ."

"Blue topaz. It opens the mind to the highest vibrations of Truth and spirituality."

"Then the pink heart-shaped one that I brought with me."

"Perhaps one can only come through the portal from that side if one is coming in the energy of Love? Interesting. Is that why you found the portal, Frankie? Did you come on a mission of Love?"

Again, Frankie thought of her strong desire to save her aunt, and that made sense. "But then there was a hole, but no stone. It was a deep hole, and shaped like a stop sign, but with six sides."

"That would be the clear quartz. It grows into points with six flat sides. And you say that stone was missing?"

Frankie nodded. She was getting the feeling that this was not such a good thing.

Unarius frowned. And when he frowned it affected the whole room. The sun seemed to withdraw, and Frankie felt that if her vision were just a little better she would see storm clouds up in the corners by the ceiling. Unarius got up from his stool and paced the length of the room and back, dodging piles of books, pinching his upper lip between his long, thin fingers, and muttering.

"That is not good, you know."

"Why not?" As she asked the question, Frankie backed up, away from Unarius and the book, and sat down on a stool a few feet away. She had the feeling she might want to be sitting down for this.

"I do not wish to scare you, Frankie, but that clear quartz probably acted like a dead-bolt lock on the door between your world and ours. You could unlock the door with the pink heart-shaped key stone that you brought with you, but when it closed behind you, the quartz would lock it again. By itself, the rose quartz would be only a weak lock, one that could easily be picked, so to speak. I would guess that someone went through the portal at some point before you did, taking that clear quartz. Then you opened the portal with the rose quartz and brought that here with you. However, if the clear quartz crystal and the rose quartz are both missing, it means that the door between the worlds is not locked at all now."

It took her a minute to understand what that might mean, but when she did, Frankie's heart started to beat very fast. Did this mean she could get back without the key stone? That she would not have to try to get the pink key stone back from Janra after all? It was too good to be true!

"Of course, now you absolutely *must* get the rose quartz stone back, and we must try to find out what happened to the clear quartz. It may just have been used and not replaced, or Janra may have gotten her hands on it somehow. But until it is back in place," Unarius told Frankie, "your world is completely unprotected. If Janra's people manage to find out where the door is, they can get through it even without the pink key stone. Even worse, if they go through and take the rose quartz with them, they can lock the door against us from that side. And that could be very unfortunate. You would not be able to get back home. And, of course, there is no telling what kind of mischief they would get into while they were there."

The Legend of Cassandra

By the time she got back to Uriel's house, Frankie felt really terrible. This was not good news. Instead of going inside right away, Frankie sat outside on the steps, trying to sort it all out. She felt guilty about wanting to stay and sad at the thought of leaving. The thought of trying to get the key stone back scared her witless. What if she couldn't get it back? And what if Janra found the doorway and invaded her grandfather's house? She had to get the key stone back and help Aunt Cassie, somehow, and do it before Janra did anything. . . but what if she couldn't?

All these warring thoughts and emotions came crashing in on her until Frankie was unable to move. Her tunic had turned a muddy-brown-red-black-blotchy color, and her stomach felt like a volcano about to erupt.

"Take those guilt and fear energies off my porch, young woman," Uriel told her sternly when she found her outside.

Frankie was lost in thought, idly twisting her aunt's necklace around her fingers and staring into the face of the woman on the medallion as if, somehow, *she* would give Frankie the answers she needed. At first she didn't hear Uriel speak to her, and then she didn't understand what she was saying.

"I told you, Frankie, I am an empath. I feel other people's emotions. I am very susceptible to those energies, Frankie," Uriel told her, "and I will not have you bringing them here. It is like bringing in the measles—only it is easier to get rid of the measles."

Frankie wasn't sure what she meant. Unarius had taught her that emotional energies are highly infectious and that people who are especially sensitive to them have to learn to recognize when they're being exposed to them. They have to protect themselves. It hadn't occurred to her that she was threatening to infect Uriel until she saw, with horror, the ugly color her tunic had become—a color that exactly reflected her thoughts and feelings. And Uriel's tunic was changing to match it.

"I'm sorry, Uriel," she said, "But Unarius told me that the lock on the door to my world is gone and Janra could invade there any minute! I just don't know what to do."

The idea of Janra's warriors rampaging through her grandfather's house the way Malus and his men had stormed through Uriel's lab made Frankie's blood run cold.

"It is only natural that you would be upset, Frankie," Uriel said, sitting down on the step beside her, "but you must know that if you focus your thoughts and emotions on the outcome you do not want, you will merely get that outcome sooner. That is the way Life works. What you resist, persists. So it behooves you to acknowledge and release your fear and then focus your attention and energy on the outcome you prefer: That your world is safe and protected. Until you are able to do that, however," she said, "take those feelings somewhere else. If you bring those doubts and fears into the house, before long we will all feel them, as well. Feelings really are infectious, you know. *You* need to feel your feelings, but *we* don't!"

"But how do I release them?" Frankie asked.

"Remember that emotions are energy. . ."

There was that energy thing again, Frankie thought.

". . . *in motion*, and let the energy move through you. Do not hang on to it. Go out on the grass and jump up and down, or pound your fist on the ground." Uriel said. "Yell, shout, do things that move the energy, that release it from your body and your energy field."

"How will I know when I've done that?" Frankie asked.

"Ah, but you will feel it," Uriel said with a wink, "and fortunately, here in Alaris, you can double-check by watching how the color of your tunic changes."

Frankie sighed, stood up, and hugged Uriel, dropping the necklace in the process. Uriel stooped to pick it up.

"Why Frankie, what is this decoration? I do not think I have seen it before. . ." she stopped in mid-sentence and peered closely at the medallion. "Why, this looks like. . . did Unarius give this to you? It almost looks like. . . Frankie, where did you get this?"

"It's my Aunt Cassie's necklace, Uriel. Isn't it nice? I'm not supposed to have it, really. It fell out of my hand and it flew through the portrait all by itself."

"This belongs to your aunt? Well, well, well," Uriel said, staring off into space with the same expression on her face that Frankie had seen come over Aunt Cassie and Unarius when they seemed to go off somewhere else. "Do you know what this is?" Uriel asked her. "It is very rare. It has the mark of the Wise Ones on it. Do you see that woman?"

Uriel leaned over and showed Frankie the woman on the medallion, the woman from the portrait. "This is Cybele, the greatest Wise One in centuries. She was the One who inherited the ancient wisdom and taught our people to use the giant crystal—you saw it, the one in the center of the city. Very few people have medallions that bear her image, Frankie. Unarius is one of them, because he is the Crystal Master of Alaris. Do you know how it came into your aunt's possession?"

"I think she got it here, Uriel," Frankie said, forgetting her troubles momentarily and catching Uriel's excitement. "She said it was like a diploma. She said she went to another world and studied about crystals and herbs and things. And when she finished studying, they gave her this." Frankie paused a second, trying to remember, then continued. "She said only two people had them, that it was very special."

"Oh, my, oh dear," said Uriel, looking at her strangely as if Frankie had said that aliens from Mars gave it to her. "You did say 'Aunt Cassie,' did you not? Oh my. I suppose that is a shortened version of Cassandra? Mmm hmmm. Cassandra. Oh yes, indeed. Oh, indeed. Cassandra and Belzar studied under Cybele and learned the secrets of the great crystals. . .," Uriel's voice took on a strange tone, as if she were reciting something that she had learned in school a long time ago. Then she snapped out of it. "Oh my. It never occurred to me that your Aunt Cassie could be. . . we must call Unarius immediately. He will not believe it. . . This adds a completely new dimension to things, to why you are here."

Uriel continued to talk, but Frankie didn't think she was really talking to her. "I wonder if Aldebaran knew? Of course, that dratted unicorn plays his own deep game and only tells what he wants to tell. He has probably known all along. Come along inside, Frankie, don't just sit there. No, wait! Run along, first, and get rid of those bad feelings before we all catch them."

Uriel did not call Unarius in the sense that Frankie was used to picking up the telephone and calling someone on it. Alarans did not need telephones, they just sent their thoughts directly to the person they had in mind. As Frankie started to concentrate on shaking off her fear and doubt, Uriel went into her lab, picked up a large clear quartz crystal and held it to her heart. Frankie knew that Uriel would merely think about Unarius, and about how she wanted him to come to the house. She would "send" those thoughts out to Unarius, and the crystal would amplify them as they went. She did this for several seconds. Then she paused, tilting her head as if listening to a response, and then she put the crystal back in its place on the table.

Within half an hour, Unarius rounded the corner and climbed the steps to the porch. Even though Frankie knew how it worked, and knew that it *did* work, each time she saw this "crystal calling," she was flabbergasted all over again.

"I brought the crystals you requested," he told Uriel when she came out to greet him. He pointed to the satchel over his shoulder.

When Frankie joined them shortly after Unarius arrived, Uriel congratulated her on the color of her tunic, a rich green, showing her newly restored sense of harmony. Frankie had been surprised at how quickly she was able to move her guilt and fear away. Her excitement about Aunt Cassie had helped to shift her energy, and then she had stomped and jumped around outside, pounding her fear under her feet into the ground, and shouting to let it out. She felt much better now, and quite pleased with herself.

Ilayna had joined them and the lab looked like Unarius and Uriel had the home movies out. There was an image being projected from something on one of the tables onto one of the blank walls. On closer inspection, Frankie saw that it was the image of a book being projected from a huge six-sided clear quartz crystal a foot high and as big around as her upper arm.

"I told you I would show you the projection crystals," Unarius said as Frankie came closer to inspect the thing, "and the perfect opportunity presented itself for us, as it always does. Sit down here, Frankie, and I will tell you all about it."

Ilayna and Frankie perched on stools, and Unarius told

them about these special projector crystals. From what he described, Frankie figured that they worked sort of like microfilm or computer disks, but with less equipment. The crystal could take a picture of each page and store it. When you wanted to look at it again, you could project the image onto a larger surface. Frankie thought it was even better than computer storage because the crystals weren't expensive and they didn't need equipment or electricity to work. And you didn't have to worry about viruses or system crashes.

"Only a few people are ever shown where these particular projector crystals are kept or how to use them," Unarius said, as he adjusted the image, "because these crystals hold the stored wisdom of the old Wise Ones of Atlantis, as well as the wisdom of the Wise Ones of Alaris through the centuries since that time. As I told you, Frankie," he added, "they do not take up as much room as books, they certainly do not weigh as much, and they do not deteriorate with time.

"When the Wise Ones realized Atlantis might be destroyed, they stored information about their civilization inside the crystals and hid them. When the crisis passed and Terra had split off from Earth, the crystals were retrieved. On your world, Frankie, Atlantis was destroyed, and the crystals remained hidden. Someday they will be found," he told her, "when the time is right, and perhaps the people will be able to use the information in different ways this time.

"Now, my friends, because of these handy crystals," Unarius told his audience, as he made a final adjustment, "we can easily refer to the legend of Cybele, Belzar, and Cassandra. Ah, here we are."

The pages with the legend were flashed up on the wall for them to read. There was a pen-and-ink drawing of Cybele — the woman in the portrait and on the necklace — and the story of her life. Cybele was in charge of the Sacred Crystals. She knew all about herbs, about the movement and influences of the planets, and about using crystals for all kinds of things, like laser beams and storing energy and information. She was a healer, too, and she taught and helped the people in Kelghard and Alaris. Often she would gaze into a crystal or a bowl of water or at a deck of cards to see a vision and be able to tell people what might be coming in their future.

"Of course," Unarius warned his audience, "true stories about a person's accomplishments can become legend, embellished and exaggerated over time. It is often difficult to sort out the simple truth.

"Legend has it that Cybele lived in the Great Forest—that is where you came into Alaris, Frankie—and people said that she knew about magical doorways to other worlds and that she spoke with the magical beasts that guarded them. One day she came to Alaris with a strange woman who wore strange clothing." He paused a minute while he changed the image on the wall to the next set of pages, and then he continued. "Everyone said she was from another world, and the village people were afraid of her. They made protective gestures whenever she walked by, and they grumbled about getting rid of her. Cybele laughed at them and pointed out that one woman was not going to conquer the city single-handed."

Unarius showed them a picture of this apparently dangerous woman. She wore blue jeans, a blue flannel shirt, and hiking boots. She was leaning against a tree, grinning, with arms folded across her chest.

"But that looks just like. . ." Frankie started to say.

"Like your Aunt Cassie? I thought so." Unarius grinned and patted her shoulder. "But wait, Frankie, there is more. And not all of it is good."

It was all laid out, there in the image on the wall. The woman known as Cassandra stayed with Cybele for many years. She and another woman studied with Cybele and learned whatever Cybele saw fit to teach them. The other woman was Belzar, one of the ruling women from Kelghard and Janra's ancestor. Cassandra and Belzar helped the people of the villages around Kelghard and taught some simple skills to those who wanted to learn them. The villages thrived.

Unfortunately it didn't last. There was a small group of people in the fortress city, who wanted power and the excitement of conquest, and who knew that some of the knowledge protected by Cybele could be turned to their own advantage, against others. After a time, Belzar fell in with this group and started planning the conquest of Alaris.

Thanks to Belzar, in addition to their fighting skills, the warriors knew how to use crystal lasers, and other forms of energy. They might have crushed Alaris. But Belzar wanted more than just an easy victory over Alaris. She wanted information and knowledge that would make her even stronger and more powerful than Cybele or the other Wise Ones, that she could use to conquer Alaris and other worlds. So she led raiding parties, stealing books and crystals in order to gain that information.

According to the legend, Cybele and Cassandra took the most important books and storage crystals and hid them in some secret caves in the mountains by the sea. And, because Belzar had threatened Cybele's life, she went into hiding, too. Cybele projected *herself* into a crystal. Cassandra hid that crystal with the others and planned to wait until it was safe to free Cybele by smashing the crystal or by projecting her out the same way Unarius was projecting the pages of the book onto the wall. Once inside the crystal, Cybele couldn't get out alone, and Cassandra was the only one who knew where she was. They assumed that Belzar's bid for power would fizzle out and die quickly. They assumed wrong.

With Cybele missing, Belzar went after Cassandra. Cassandra had also been trained to fight and, because it was unavoidable, one day she stood up against Belzar, and the two women fought their decisive battle alone in a clearing in the forest. That battle became the stuff of legends. Some accounts said that it lasted for five days. Some said that the entire forest shook from the force of sword against sword. Both women knew how to call down the energy and use it, and their battle was marked by thunder and lightning above the forest that everyone for miles could see.

"To this day people argue over who won," Unarius said. "But regardless of who won, the war between Kelghard and Alaris ended with that battle, and both women were badly wounded. Cassandra was seen riding a huge white horse into the forest. But that was the last time Cassandra was ever seen. Belzar dragged herself back to Kelghard to die, but she claimed victory because Cassandra had disappeared. There were rumors later that Belzar claimed that she had trapped Cassandra in a crystal, where she would remain forever."

"But that's not true!" Frankie jumped up and yelled, trying to set the story straight. "I saw them! Aunt Cassie beat her! And it wasn't a horse she was riding, it was a unicorn—three times bigger and fiercer than Aldebaran! I saw it! I was there!"

"*You were there??*" The other three asked in unison.

"Yes. Well, no. I mean. . . " Frankie blushed a little bit, and felt a little self conscious about her outburst. She wondered if they would believe her or think she was crazy. "Well, I wasn't really there, physically. But it was the strangest thing. The night before I came here, I woke up from a nightmare, but it seemed like more than a nightmare, if you know what I mean. It felt real. It was a nightmare of Aunt Cassie on a giant white unicorn fighting another woman. They had ice spears and shields and they threw lightning from their fingers. They even wore leather clothes like Malus wore. I saw it all. I was sitting on the fence, watching. And she said. . . oh, my. . . she said that I couldn't sit on the fence much longer, that I might have to fight soon because she was too weak to go on."

"But what do you suppose happened to her?" Ilayna asked.

"According to the book," Unarius answered, "Cassandra went to the crystal cave and put herself into one of the crystals, just as Cybele had done. Perhaps Belzar found that crystal?"

"But then she couldn't have come home," Frankie cried. "And she *did* come home—at least most of her did! She's been sick for two years. She told me that she had left part of herself here. How could that happen?"

"Maybe she tried to project herself into a crystal, but she was caught in the middle of the process," Uriel said. "Part of her might have been trapped in the crystal, though, and when Cassandra finally made her way to the door between the worlds, that small part was left behind."

"Or," Unarius added, "she may have put herself into a crystal that was later broken somehow, so that most of her was released but part of her remained in the crystal."

"It all seems so strange, though," Uriel said. "We know that Cybele actually existed and disappeared, but we always thought these other stories were invented to explain a tragic death. We never thought they were literally true. I wonder if there really are some secret caves? And I wonder if those projector crystals—and Cybele—are still there?"

"And part of Aunt Cassie, too!" Frankie added. She, too, wondered about those caves and whether she could find them.

❧ 8 ❧

The Crystal Cave

*T*he sun was barely up when Frankie left the house the next morning. She wasn't exactly sneaking out before Uriel and Ilayna got up, but she wasn't exactly announcing her departure, either. She would have liked to invite Ilayna to come with her, but she was sure Ilayna would have told Uriel, and then things might have gotten complicated. She wanted to see those caves, and she wanted to see them before anyone stopped her or anyone else got to them. So she wasn't taking any chances.

Frankie packed her provisions carefully: two large quartz crystals that store light and can be set to shine like flashlights, a digging tool that Uriel used in the garden, a thick towel that might come in handy, paper and pencil for taking notes, a large jug of fresh water, two apples, and three tomato and cheese sandwiches wrapped in a napkin. She was afraid to wear her sweater, jeans and sneakers, because someone might see her in them. So she added them to the other provisions in the heavy cotton backpack she found in the closet, thinking they might come in handy, too.

With only a vague idea of where she was going, Frankie

ate a quick and quiet breakfast and set out toward the range of mountains across the valley. She was sure that if she could find the caves, the crystals would still be there — including the one that held part of her Aunt Cassie. After all, even Uriel and Unarius had never imagined that the caves in the old story ever really existed. But Frankie was sure that they existed and that she would find them. The projector crystal had given a vague description of the caves' location. Now all she had to do was reach the sea cliffs and find a rock formation that might be called Cybele's Altar. Those rocks would point the way to the caves.

By noon she was climbing on the cliffs and she had exchanged her sandals for her sneakers because she needed better traction on the rocks. It was unlikely that anyone would see her, because it looked like she was completely alone on these rocks, except for the birds. More than once, Frankie saw a hawk or an eagle swoop and soar across the bright sky, and she stopped her climbing in mid-step to watch their perfect grace. But the sun was beating down on her, there was no shade, and her head was beginning to throb. She was starting to feel tired and hungry, and she was beginning to wish she had taken Ilayna into her confidence and brought her along for the company. She found a series of flat rock ledges and smoothed the dirt and bracken off one with her hand. She sat down, opened her pack, and rationed out one sandwich, one apple, and a cupful of water.

Eating lunch revived her spirits and eased her headache. From her perch Frankie could see back across the entire valley. She thought she could see Uriel's house and the pond beyond it. And she could see the forested hills on the other side of the valley that separated Alaris from Janra's fortress city, Kelghard. But Frankie wasn't sure which way to turn.

She had climbed a considerable distance without seeing anything that looked like the entrance to a cave. What if the caves were down at sea level? The legend in the projector crystal wasn't very specific. It merely said that Cybele's Altar guarded the entrance. And it didn't go into any detail about where she'd find the Altar or what it looked like. What if the entrance to the crystal caves was blocked or under water? The path had stopped at the rock ledges. She could continue to climb up the rocks, or try to go back down, and neither way looked particularly easy or promising. She had thought a search for the caves would be fun and exciting. Instead, it was hot, tiring, and frustrating. She was bored with it. She wanted to go home.

But she was not ready to give up yet. Frankie decided to work with what Uriel and Aldebaran had taught her. She would focus on what she wanted: finding the caves. She sat for a few minutes, trying to visualize the entrance to the caves, trying to feel how she would feel when she found it. She *intended* to find it. She *expected* to find it, and her heart filled with that expectation. When she stopped focusing on that after a few minutes, Frankie wasn't sure if it had worked, but she felt more optimistic and ready to give it another try, to search one more time to find another path before giving up.

She was kneeling on the ledge re-packing the backpack when a huge brown hawk swooped past her so closely she could make out the individual feathers on its wing. She shrank back against the rock face behind her, losing her grip on the backpack. It rolled down to the right, completely off the ledge and down the side of a huge rock face, nestling into a hole about 20 feet below her. She couldn't leave it down there because it had all of her supplies in it, including her jeans and sweater, which she had planned to put on before continuing her climb. Even though the sneakers helped keep her footing on the rocks, her short tunic and bare legs made her feel vulnerable and awkward. Her legs were already scraped and bleeding in a couple of places from her efforts.

She took a deep breath and then scrambled down across the rocks after the backpack. Each step took her farther from the safety of the ledge, and with each step it was harder to find a foothold among the rocks. The ground was steeply sloped and covered in gravel, and she clung desperately to scrubby bushes and lifeless tree limbs as she lurched downward, terrified that she would lose her footing and be swept along with the gravel as it plummeted downward. She finally saw a second ledge directly below and she held her breath, sent up a little prayer, and allowed herself to drop down onto it. It was wider than she had thought, and Frankie heaved a sigh of relief. From here she could reach the backpack, and then climb back up to the other ledge.

She retrieved the backpack, straightened up, and was so startled by what she saw that she almost dropped it again. A scroungy, withered brown shrub grew up through a crevice in the rock directly in her path. Behind that shrub was exactly what she had been looking for: a third ledge, about 10 feet away, with tall rock outcroppings on each side that made it look like a flat altar with two candles. This must be Cybele's Altar! Forgetting all about putting on her jeans and sweater, she slung the backpack over her shoulder and crawled across the rock to reach it.

The Altar marked the entrance of a cave, an entrance that was now so overgrown with gnarly trees and scraggly shrubs that she would never have seen it from above or below. If she hadn't dropped her backpack, she would never have found it. Frankie remembered Uriel telling her that quite often something that seemed bad—like dropping her backpack—could turn out to be the best thing that could possibly happen. Sometimes the good part is obvious right away, and sometimes you have to look for it. Frankie was glad that this time it was obvious. It was as if that hawk had known she was 20 feet too high and had swooped down on her to force her down to where she needed to be. Was it just a coincidence? Or had her effort to visualize herself finding the cave, and her active intent to find it, put something in motion to help her do it?

Frankie gave a joyful "whoop!" and, in her mind, she thanked the hawk for helping her. She took one of the big quartz flashlight crystals out of her pack, held it against her forehead and mentally asked it to light, as Unarius had taught her. Then she stepped through the curtain of branches into the cave.

♥　　♥　　♥

It was dark, dank and musty inside. Within a few steps, the soft quartz beam revealed a narrow rock-strewn path that led off to the right, and Frankie headed in that direction. She slowly picked her way among loose rocks, holes, and spider webs, and she was reminded again why she had always hated summer camp. The sight of a rat the size of a small dog almost made her turn and run, but she told herself that the rat was more scared of her than she was of it. She hoped she was right. Besides, she was on a mission, and she had come too far to turn back now just because of a stupid rat. She gritted her teeth and kept going.

After what felt like hours of inching along in the dark with only the glow of the crystal to light her way, Frankie came to a place where three tunnels came together. She wasn't sure which way to go, but something deep inside her urged her toward the one on the left. She remembered what Uriel had told her about her heart always knowing what to do, so she went with it. After a few hesitant steps, she felt sure she had taken the right path. The path started to get wider and she continued along. She turned a corner and suddenly a hundred yards ahead of her the tunnel opened out into a huge glittering cavern that stretched out above and below her like a giant subway station.

Steps that had been cut into the rock led down to the cavern floor, where a stream flowed out toward the sea. The huge cavern seemed to be cut out of living crystal. Light from some unknown source sparkled and flashed off the ceiling and walls, filling the whole cavern with bright streaks of purple, green and white light. This had to be it!

Frankie scrambled down the carved-out steps all the way to the bottom, almost falling a few times as she tried to take it all in. She spotted a small cave on the other side of the stream that looked like it was filled to overflowing with crystals and gems of all sizes, colors and shapes. Crossing the stream at its narrowest point, she headed straight for it. She was sure she would find those special crystals here.

The small crystal cave was even better at close range. Gems and crystals seemed to pour out of the walls, filling the cavern. No one was around, but here and there Frankie could see the traces of human presence: a pick and shovel were propped up against the near wall and there were several sacks, some filled, some empty, as if someone had been sorting the stones. Frankie retrieved the second crystal torch from her backpack, activated it, and set the two of them up on a flat rock. She was almost blinded as the reflected light of their beams filled the small chamber.

"Well, well, well, what 'ave we here?"

The voice was rough and gravelly, and the tone set her heart racing as Frankie spun around at the unexpected sound.

"Who are you?" she demanded, planting her hands on her hips and masking her sudden terror with bravado.

"I might ask ye the same," the man said. "Ye be trespassing on my mistress Janra's property, and I'd like to know who ye are, why ye're here, and how ye got here."

The man was dressed like Malus had been, in leather

leggings and jerkin, but he was shorter and heavier than Malus and somehow looked harder and meaner.

"I'm from Alaris," Frankie said, hoping to be sent off without any further problems. "I climbed the rocks and found a cave. I was just exploring,"

"Alaris, eh?" The coarse man hawked and spat. "Them folk from Alaris wouldn't go to the trouble of climbing any rocks. They's busy thinking big thoughts, not doing big things. So why would ye go a-climbin'? And what are those things on ye feet?"

Frankie couldn't think of anything to say to him, to explain away her sneakers, but her anger was quickly overtaking her fear. Who was *he*, anyway? And who did he think he was to treat her this way? She hated bullies more than anything else, and this man was just one more bully. It was the one thing that could really make her mad. "It's none of your business, you jerk!" she snapped at him. "Besides, this isn't Kelghard, it's Alaris. Janra doesn't own this cave!"

"And what's in 'ere?" He said, ignoring her outburst. He picked up the backpack she had dropped and rummaged through it. He pulled out a leg of her jeans and held the material out to her. "What's this? I be thinkin' my mistress might be very interested in you and yer strange things."

"Well, your mistress isn't going to see anything!" Frankie snapped, snatching the backpack out of his hands and slinging it back over her shoulder. "You have *no right*. . ."

She stopped in mid-sentence with a gasp as she felt her arms being caught up behind her in someone else's strong, rough hands. And in that moment, she knew that she was sunk.

The Queen of Everything

"So, you have been hearing the same stories I have," Janra said with a sneer as she loomed over her captive, "all about caves by the sea and hidden magic crystals. It is unfortunate for you that I got there first. My men are emptying those caves of crystals and bringing them here to one of my storage rooms. Who knows what I might find?"

Frankie had a pretty good idea what she might find, but she didn't say anything. She just shrank back in her chair and tried to keep from screaming. She had heard about Janra, of course, but she wasn't at all prepared for the real thing. This woman standing arrogantly in front of her was about six feet tall, with thick black hair pulled back and secured behind her neck in a leather tie, leaving a thick tail hanging down her back to her waist. She wore the same type of leather garments as her men, who were cringing against the wall, just as Frankie was cringing back in her chair. The only difference was that Janra had a design pressed into the leather across her chest—a design very similar to the picture of the woman on Aunt Cassie's necklace. She looked entirely too much like the warrior in Frankie's dream, the one Uriel had called Belzar.

Back in the cave, the men had tied Frankie's hands and feet and loaded her into a small wooden sailboat hidden just inside an entrance to the cave where the stream met the sea. She didn't know how long the sea journey to Janra's fortress took, but to Frankie it felt like days. She suddenly really regretted that she hadn't told anyone where she was going, and she had never felt so scared and alone in all her life. She didn't need to see the color of her tunic to know that she was stewing in fear.

The men had thrown her into a tiny cabin like a sack of potatoes and left her there to worry about what they were going to do to her. Thoughts of escape were useless, of course. Even if she could get her hands and feet untied, she would not get far from a boat in the middle of the sea. She was a mediocre swimmer, at best.

So she lay there and concentrated on taking slow, deep breaths to calm herself, which was not easy, considering that the ship creaked and moaned as if its very planks would pull apart before her eyes and leave her drowning in a pile of rotted wood. The ship held its own, though, despite its groaning, and they finally docked. She was shoved down the gangway onto a landing where horses awaited them, and she was thrown up onto the saddle in front of one of the men. They rode through thick forest until they reached the fortress.

Frankie barely got more than a glimpse of the huge stone fortress before they pushed her inside through a heavy door in a round tower at one of the corners, and up several winding flights of stairs. She had seen enough, though, to realize that this was indeed a fortress, a fortress well protected by a large number of armed guards. And she wondered how she would ever escape.

Frankie was sick, tired, and terrified by the time they left her alone to wait for their mistress Janra to come and decide her fate. Until now, Frankie's time in Alaris had been an exciting adventure. She had made new friends, learned new skills, and had a good time. Now, though, she realized what Aunt Cassie had meant when she said it might be dangerous to come here. Now, the danger seemed all too real.

At least they hadn't left her in the dungeon! As she looked around, Frankie felt like she had somehow traveled back through time and dropped into some sort of medieval castle. The roaring fire in the fireplace at one end of the room barely took the chill off the thick stone walls, and the warmth hovered under the high, beamed ceiling. The furniture was plain, carved wood, but it was not as primitive as Frankie would have expected from the mental image she had formed of these barbarians. To be honest, she hadn't actually pictured them living indoors at all. The walls were hung with huge tapestries and decorated with weapons, mostly swords and shields. All, that is, except for the wall opposite the fireplace, which held a giant life-size portrait of a woman—a woman who looked like the warrior on the giant black stallion in Frankie's dream, a woman who wore a necklace just like Aunt Cassie's. Could it be. . .?

"She's hard to ignore, isn't she?" Janra asked as she strode into the room and stood preening in front of the portrait. "That is Belzar, the first of my people to learn the secrets of Alaris from one of the wise ones. She was famous for her many battles. She was so powerful that it took a being from another world to even match her in a terrible battle that mortally wounded Belzar and killed the other."

Janra paced back and forth in front of the portrait, slapping a short riding whip against her leg as she went. "But those powers didn't die when she did, they were passed down from generation to generation to the women rulers of Kelghard. And some of us have gone to Alaris, and other places, to learn more." She whirled around and stopped dead in front of Frankie. "So do not underestimate me, girl! I will turn you into a dog or some other mindless beast, if you don't do as I say."

Frankie didn't doubt it for a minute, especially after Janra threw a few sparks of orange lightning from her fingertips into the fireplace, causing the flames to leap up and crackle. The men behind her made a strange gesture with their hands to ward off evil. It was the same gesture they had used when Uriel called down the thunder and lightening the night Malus came and stole the pink key stone. Janra may understand power and magic, Frankie thought, but her followers clearly didn't. They were terrified of her, and Frankie thought that Janra liked it that way.

If Frankie had not been so scared, she might have thought about trying to find the key stones. They must be somewhere in the fortress, after all, and she had certainly solved the problem of getting inside! Instead, it was all she could do to keep from screaming, all she could do to keep her hand wrapped tightly around the strap of her backpack, which she'd pushed under her chair and was trying to hide with her feet. The men had brought it along with them, but Frankie wasn't sure if that was a blessing or a curse. She might be able to figure out some plausible lie about the tennis shoes she was wearing, but if Janra saw her jeans and sweater, there was no telling what might happen. Even worse if she saw Aunt Cassie's necklace, which Frankie had put in the backpack for safe-keeping. If Janra saw those things, it would only be a question of time before she figured out that Frankie not only knew where the door was to the other world, but that she had actually come through it. And Frankie didn't want to be within grabbing distance when Janra figured that out. She closed her eyes and sent out a mental cry for help to Uriel, to Unarius, to Aldebaran, to *anybody*. She even called on that hawk for help.

"Now, I want to know what you were doing in my cave." Janra's voice was cold and hard as steel as she stood directly in front of Frankie's chair, not two feet away, and glared down at her from her considerable height. Her left hand clutched the whip, while her right hand clenched and unclenched at her side, as if it had a will of its own. Frankie didn't want to think about what that hand might want to do. She noticed that Janra's fingernails were long and curved. She figured they would be lethal, even without the lightning she had seen Janra throw from her fingers.

"I'm talking to you, girl," Janra sneered, taking a step closer.

"I was just looking," Frankie said, speaking faster than usual, as if her words were the only thing that would keep Janra back. "You're right. I heard the legens, and I wondered if I could find the caves. That's all. I've always been too curious for my own good. I didn't mean any harm."

"Ha!" Janra laughed, flicking the whip a little too close to Frankie's chin. "As if *you* could do any harm! You're nothing but a little gnat—a mere annoyance to me."

"The feel of a good cutting edge might make her talk, Mistress," one of the men said, stepping forward as he pulled a knife from a scabbard at his side.

Janra whirled around and sent a flash of lightning searing into his right wrist. He dropped the knife as smoke rose from a jagged gash in his flesh. He quickly grabbed a bandana from around his neck and wrapped it around the wound, then cradled his hand against his chest.

"You know better than to anticipate me, Caius," Janra shouted at her man. Then she turned back to Frankie with a low, sinister purr: "We don't need to resort to knives just yet, now, do we?"

As if in answer, Frankie felt the hair on the back of her neck stand straight up, and she shrank back farther in the chair, trying to get away. None of the experiences in her life had prepared her for something like this. She felt small and insignificant, like a beetle about to be crushed under someone's boot, and she had absolutely no idea what to do.

"Now then," Janra continued. She put one foot up on Frankie's leg as if it were a stool. She leaned forward, resting one arm across her knee. She pointed down to the floor. "I want to know about these interesting shoes on your feet. We have nothing like them here in Kelghard. They're rather ugly, aren't they? Is this the new fashion in Alaris?"

"It's just something new. I don't like them much, either," Frankie lied. "They're stupid. You can have them if you want. Or we could just throw them away or something." She knew she was babbling, but she couldn't stop herself.

Janra ignored her. She put her foot on the floor and reached down and retrieved the backpack, wrenching it out of Frankie's grasp and dropping it on a nearby table. "And what might be in here that's new and interesting from Alaris?" Frankie couldn't stifle a gasp.

"That's mine," Frankie shouted without thinking, as she made an unsuccessful grab for it. "You leave that alone!" As soon as the words came out, Frankie knew she'd made a horrible mistake.

Without any visible effort, Janra reached over and grabbed Frankie by the neck. She started to squeeze, smiling down at Frankie as she did so, as if nothing out of the ordinary was going on. She lifted her arm up, and Frankie rose up out of her chair, dangling by the neck from Janra's outstretched hand. It hurt like crazy, and Frankie wondered fleetingly how long it would take for her neck to break. Her head swam and she started to see all kinds of images behind her eyes—sparks and stars of various colors. She couldn't breathe and she knew she would pass out soon if Janra didn't release the pressure.

Finally, Janra let go and Frankie dropped like a load of wash into the chair, with her head rolling forward. She didn't know if she'd ever feel right again.

"Well, I wonder what's in this fascinating bag?" Janra crooned. She turned to the five men who were still in the room, lined up uneasily against one wall. "There must be something very valuable here, if she is so desperate to protect it, don't you think? It must contain wonderful magical things that Janra would like to have."

They all nodded and murmured, apparently just as terrified as Frankie and equally unsure about what Janra would do next.

Janra pulled Frankie up from her chair and over to the table, ordering her to empty the backpack. Frankie froze, staring down at it, dreading the moment when she had to reveal its contents. The denim jeans and sweater would be a dead giveaway, but Frankie was more afraid that Janra would see Aunt Cassie's necklace. She would recognize it, Frankie was sure. And then Frankie would *really* have some explaining to do. As Janra urged her on, Frankie pulled the things out of her bag as slowly as she possibly could—first the towel, then a crystal flashlight, then a sandwich in a small bag, then the other crystal flashlight—and all the time her mind worked furiously to try to figure out a way to conceal her clothes and the necklace from the woman.

Frankie had realized she could hide the necklace in an inner pocket of the bag, but hadn't come up with a way to conceal the blue jeans, when she heard a big commotion in the hallway outside.

As she tried desperately to stall, Frankie was astonished to see Ilayna and a strange woman enter the room, followed by a dozen men in blue uniforms. Janra's men fell back out of the way, but their faces didn't show any fear.

"Well, well, well," Janra said. "If it isn't my dear sister, Aradia. . . and my dear niece. What could possibly bring you here today?" She turned to Frankie, and Frankie could almost see a dark thunder cloud gathering above Janra's head. "News travels fast in these parts," Janra said with false sweetness. "It appears that our guest just happens to know my sister. I wonder why she forgot to mention that?" She looked at Frankie in a way that made it clear what people meant when they said, "if looks could kill."

Ilayna stepped forward and hugged her aunt, who stiffened slightly, before walking over to place herself next to Frankie at the table. "Hello, Aunt Janra. It's wonderful to see you, too. I'm sorry if my friend displeased you in some way."

The air in the room felt leaden, and it felt like no one breathed. Janra didn't reply, so Ilayna continued, turning toward Frankie and her mother. "Aunt Janra, mother," Ilayna said it a formal tone, "I would like to present my friend, Frances Maxwell. She's just recently come to Alaris to study with grandfather and Uriel. Frankie, you've met my Aunt Janra,"

"Queen of Kelghard," Janra said quickly, as if concerned that Ilayna might not get it right.

"And this is my mother," Ilayna continued, "Aradia, her Majesty Janra's sister, Princess of Kelghard." Ilayna then stepped back toward the door.

Frankie rose at the introduction, feeling a bit less terrified, now that help had arrived. As she rose, Janra stepped back a few paces, keeping her gaze on Frankie's face.

The other woman, a smaller, lighter version of Janra, made a slight bow and smiled in Frankie's direction, acknowledging the introduction. But most of her attention was turned toward Janra, as if looking for signs of an imminent explosion. She was dressed in a dark blue dress and looked much more like the lady of the manor than her sister did.

"I gather this is a mischievous friend of Ilayna's, Janra," Aradia said smoothly, as if this sort of thing happened every day. She walked across the room and stood between Janra and Frankie, drawing Frankie to her side within the curve of an arm around her shoulders. "She became excited by some of those old stories. You know the ones I mean. And then she got lost in the caves. Ilayna has come to fetch her home again." Aradia nudged Frankie toward the door.

"Thanks for finding her for us, Aunt Janra," Ilayna said sweetly, already heading for the door and tugging on Frankie's arm to pull her along. "We'll keep a better eye on her from now on, so she won't go where she shouldn't."

Janra looked around at them all—her own men, Frankie, Ilayna, Aradia, and Aradia's men—and the whole room seemed to take in a deep breath and hold it, waiting to see what she would do. Nothing and no one moved. Finally, Janra did.

"Ha!" she laughed, slapping the whip handle against her thigh. "I suppose you think you've outsmarted me this time?" She walked over to Frankie and waived the coiled whip in her face. When Janra continued speaking, they were standing toe to toe. "Don't believe for a minute that you have outmaneuvered me, child. I will let you go now because it suits me to do so. But I *will* get my answers out of you, young one, when I'm good and ready. There is more to you than meets the eye, and I intend to find out what it is—at my leisure. There's something about that hair, too. I've seen that red hair before. You know it and I know it. And next time, my dear sister and my niece will not show up to help you. Next time it will be just you and me. Do you understand?"

As the hair all over her body stood on end, Frankie understood all too well. She rushed back to the table, grabbed her backpack, and headed back out the door as Ilayna and Aradia closed in behind her. She didn't exactly run down the hall and away from her tormentor, but she didn't dawdle, either, as she followed Aradia and Ilayna through a labyrinth of hallways and stairwells.

At the stables, Aradia helped the two girls mount horses

and she bid them farewell. Five of her own trusted men would deliver them to Alaris, and to Uriel.

Frankie longed for a soothing bath and a warm bed. She still felt shocked and terrified by her encounter with Janra and, after she made Ilayna tell her all about the rescue, she sank into a mood of dark despair as they rode home to Alaris. She hadn't accomplished anything by going to the caves. She hadn't found the crystal for her aunt and she hadn't found the pink key stone. All she had done was prove to herself how terrifying Janra was and how silly she had been to think for a minute that she could accomplish her mission. And all she could really think about was what might happen if she ever came face to face with Janra again.

❧ 10 ❧

Mind Over Matter

Uriel welcomed them home with hugs and great
mounds of baked goods.

"I thought you said you weren't worried," Ilayna
teased her, knowing that baking was Uriel's way of
keeping her hands busy while she put her mind to some
problem.

"When I looked in my crystal and saw the image of
Frankie being dumped into that boat, I just could not help
myself," Uriel laughed, her cheeks and tunic tinged pink with
relief. "Even though I was absolutely certain that all would be
well, because it always is, one way or another." She gathered
Frankie up in a big hug and then offered the girls a vast array
of sandwiches, muffins, brownies, and cakes. "Certainty is
good, but actually having you back home safe is even better."

But Frankie knew that she was not "home safe." Her trip
to the fortress and her confrontation with Janra had scared her
to the core of her being. This was no television or storybook
adventure. Janra, the six-foot warrior in leather garments, with
her knives and swords and magical powers, was *real*. That
huge stone fortress with heavily armed guards all over the

place was *real*. It probably had a very real dungeon, and there was a very real possibility that she could end up spending time in it.

Frankie was scared. She was terrified at the thought of going back there to try to get the key stone back, terrified that Janra would be ready and waiting for her when she tried. But the door between the worlds was unlocked and unprotected without the key stones, and she couldn't let the terror of Janra and her warriors get into her grandfather's house, into her world. Somehow, Frankie swore to herself, she'd get those crystal keys back and lock that door between worlds once and for all. Somehow, she'd find a way to stop Janra in her tracks. She knew that she had to work fast, though. She didn't think Janra would wait for her to fall into her hands again. Janra was very likely to come after her. And next time she probably wouldn't get off so easy!

This was a turning point for Frankie, and she started taking her situation very seriously. Before dinner every night, Ilayna gave her lessons in how to become invisible. The two girls also practiced summoning energy and hurling it from their fingertips, the way Frankie had seen Janra do it. They didn't get very far, though. They had to stop their experiments after she singed Sebastian's tail by mistake.

Frankie spent her days studying with Unarius, learning to do all those things he had demonstrated for her. She learned to move things by just thinking about it, to "sense" other people's thoughts, and to "see" across time and space by using her mental vision or by looking into a piece of black glass, a crystal ball, or a bowl of water. She also learned to read *auras*, the energy fields of people and animals, and to know things about people by the color of their aura. She asked Unarius why it was that people in Alaris worked with energy this way, but people in her world didn't. If she could be taught to do it, why hadn't other people learned?

"Everyone has these abilities," Unarius told her, "even in your world. They are perfectly natural, like vision or hearing. It may be that the knowledge was kept secret, so that only a few could benefit by using it. Or the knowledge may have been lost altogether. I believe that people who discover these abilities and openly use them are often viewed with suspicion, denounced as witches or sorcerers, or worse."

"Or kooks," Frankie added, "that's what my Dad calls them."

"Or kooks," Unarius agreed, smiling at it, "but everyone really does have these abilities—they have probably just become latent through lack of use. They are like muscles: If you do not use them for a time, they get stiff and hard to use. But as you start using them, they get stronger."

Unarius gave Frankie a headband that helped her learn to work with the energies and strengthened these senses that she had never used. It was a silver band with a large clear crystal about the size of a quarter set right in the middle. It looked sort of like other headbands she had at home, but this one she wore across her forehead like a visor, instead of across the top of her head to hold her hair back out of the way. The crystal was set so it fell right in the center of her forehead, over what Unarius called her third eye. It was supposed to help her with all kinds of energy exercises. It could help focus a thought like a laser beam so she could watch it spin out from her head into the air. It also worked like a television or radio tuner to help her "tune in" and recognize the different energies around her or even tune in to other people's thoughts.

Frankie thought it was like having training wheels on a bike: Once she learned to see and use the energies on her own, she wouldn't need the headband.

They started with *telekinesis*—moving things with your mind—because Unarius told her it was the easiest way to learn how to focus and concentrate a thought. Frankie sat at the end of one of the long tables in the workroom and Unarius set up various small items at the other end: a pencil, a few small stones, a little ball. She was supposed to mentally move them or, as he put it, "talk" to the atoms and suggest that they move. He made it sound so easy. And when he showed her, it looked easy.

Frankie sat and thought at those little things at the end of the table as hard as she could, holding her breath and screwing her eyes up into her head, making all kinds of faces that showed how hard she was concentrating. But nothing happened. She tried it again—longer, harder, and with more funny faces—and still nothing happened.

She couldn't get them to move for anything. Finally, when she could see dull brownish gray wisps of annoyance and frustration rising up around her to match the new color of her tunic, Unarius told her to go home.

"My dear," he said, "look at you! Look at this thick cloud of anger and frustration all around you. Do you know why you are feeling this way?"

"Well, I have to learn to do this, and I can't," Frankie said. "I feel like a failure."

"Ah, I see!" Unarius said. He sat down on a stool next to her and tapped his finger on the smooth surface of the table. "If this were just a game—if this were something that we played at and we said, 'Oh, let us just try this and see what happens'—would you feel frustrated?"

"No, because I wouldn't think I had to get it right, but was doing it wrong," Frankie answered. "So I wouldn't think I'd failed."

"Because if it was just something we played with, you would not feel that you *had* to be able to do it, perfectly and immediately. Is that right?"

Frankie nodded.

"Ah, my dear," he said, reaching over to take her hands in

his. "Can you try to not beat yourself up so much? Can you try to let yourself learn things playfully, without criticism and judgment of yourself? This is not a test!"

"I know it's not a test," Frankie protested, "but I have to learn how to do this. I have to stop Janra."

"I know, dear," he said, "but you must let yourself off the hook just a little, if you can, and take some of the pressure off yourself. You will learn it faster and easier and better if you relax and play with it."

Frankie didn't feel convinced. It was obvious to her that he just wasn't understanding how important this was or how hard it was for her.

He pointed to the dull brownish black cloud that rose up around her head, which she could see with the help of the headband. "The best thing about being able to see these clouds around yourself is that it gives you a flag, a warning that something is out of balance. Emotions do not attack us, they help us. They let us know when something needs our attention. A feeling of happiness or joy lets us know that everything is just fine. But what about fear? If you feel afraid, it does not mean that you are a coward. It means that there is probably something going on that needs your attention. Your emotions are sort of tapping you on your shoulder and saying, 'make sure you notice this thing over here.'" He tapped her shoulder to illustrate his point.

"Perhaps you had not noticed that rattle snake over there, or perhaps you are climbing and you need to watch your footing carefully. Fear's tap on the shoulder makes you pause and look around to see what needs your attention or what might be wrong. But emotions are energies in motion. They need to move. If you notice them and you ask them what they are trying to show you, then they can tell you and move on. But if you do not let emotions have their say, if you pretend they are not there because you don't like the way they make you feel, they will stick around, form a dark cloud around you and make you feel bad. And if they get stuck for too long, they can even turn into disease. *Dis-ease*. Do you understand?"

Frankie wasn't exactly sure, but she thought she understood the general idea. It was sort of like dealing with her little brother, Sam. Frankie knew that when he wanted attention, the fastest way to get rid of him was to stop what she was doing and listen to him. Once he knew that he could get her attention, get her to listen to him, he'd go away. But if she ignored him, he would try increasingly annoying ways to demand her attention—he'd pull her hair, grab her book, or kick her in the shin.

Frankie tried to ask her anger and frustration what it was trying to tell her. Maybe this was a warning that she was trying too hard, putting too much pressure on herself, like Unarius said? Maybe this was really self-doubt and fear that she would fail? When that thought floated into her mind, her whole body seemed to say *yes* in a big sigh of relief. Unarius was right: When she paid attention to her feelings—when she listened to them and really allowed herself to feel her feelings— then they seemed to let go and move on.

"Frustration is a difficult emotion, of course," Unarius said, "because it means you are expecting something that is not happening. The easiest way to help that one move along is to make your expectations a little more realistic and relax a bit. And remember—when you have these feelings and a dark cloud around yourself, you are also sharing them with everyone around you."

The last remnants of the dark cloud dispersed, and Frankie felt lighter and happier. And then a strange thought occurred to her. "Unarius," she asked, "do we have these thought-and-emotion clouds at home, too?" she asked.

"I would think that it is likely," he answered, "and it is also likely much worse there, because your people do not know about them and do not do anything to consciously change their thoughts and emotions to keep them positive or clear the negative ones away."

Picking up on that idea, Unarius went over to a big board and started drawing a bunch of people with clouds over their heads. "Imagine hundreds of people, all walking around together with clouds of anger, fear, frustration, and pain floating around them. As contagious as those emotions are, everyone they encounter will start to feel them, and each of them will start trailing a dark cloud around with them, too. Finally, their combined dark clouds would be so dark and so thick that no one could escape—and everyone would be feeling all those terrible emotions, the anger, fear, frustration and pain, all the time."

It made her shudder to think about it, but Frankie thought it made sense. Most of the time lately she could almost see the dark cloud around her father, even without her new crystal headband! No wonder people at home did not seem very happy to her—maybe they were all running around wrapped up in black clouds of pain and fear and doubt.

Frankie was lost in thought as she sat down at the table again and, only paying half attention to them, she mentally dismissed the objects at the end of the table. To her surprise, they shot off the table, one after another, and ricocheted around the room. Frankie burst out laughing and Unarius scrambled to catch them.

"Well, there you go," he said, patting her shoulder. "I knew you could do it. And very well, too. You might try having a bit more faith in yourself, you know, and relax and enjoy your studies more. When you put so much pressure on yourself, it only makes it harder. When you fear you cannot do a thing, it is likely that you will prove yourself right. It is so much easier when you just assume that you *can* do something, and then allow yourself to do it. Now that you have mastered telekinesis, let us move on to some minor mind reading."

"But Unarius," Frankie laughed, "it's wonderful that I did it, but I don't know *how* I did it! What, exactly, did I *do*?"

Unarius laughed back, "Why Frankie, you listened to your fear and let it go. Then you stopped *trying* to make it happen and you just *let it happen*. Didn't I already say that?"

Unarius was right. The secret, she realized, was to not *try* so hard. Instead of moving on to something else right away, Frankie practiced moving small items, then moved up to bigger ones until she could mentally untie a knot in a piece of rope at the end of the table or deliver Unarius' cup of tea from the table to his hand across the room without spilling a drop. And each time, she just had to *not try*. Instead of fearing that it wouldn't work, that she wouldn't be able to do it, she had to just *know* it would work. She realized there was a difference, too, between hoping and knowing. She had to *expect* it to work. She slowly developed her own technique of sort of unfocusing her eyes and looking kind of sideways and thinking of something else. Then, it would work. And once she *knew* it would work, it was easy.

Over the course of the next few days, Frankie moved from objects to animals. She did not exactly move them with her mind, but she learned to influence their minds with hers. Unarius said it was a combination of telekinesis and telepathy. The cat Sebastian finally refused to go anywhere near her because she kept sending him to the kitchen for food that wasn't there. She made it up to him with a big bowl of treats.

From there, she moved to real telepathy and reading minds. Frankie soon realized that it was not really a case of reading someone's mind, it was more like sensing or moving into a person's aura or energy field and recognizing the thoughts and emotions she found there.

"Everyone has an energy field," Unarius told her. "So you just reach out with your energy field and touch into theirs."

Unarius taught her to become very, very still, and begin to feel for a part of her that wasn't physical that extended outside her physical body. When she was able to identify it, she was amazed to feel how far from her body her energy field extended. Then, Frankie would imagine a finger of her own energy reaching out to Unarius. He helped her at first by concentrating on an image of something in his own mind that would cause him to have an emotional response. It was especially easy when he recalled when she was kidnapped and taken to Janra: Frankie's energy would touch his and jump back because of the strong concern that she could feel there. Not only could she feel his feelings about it, she could also see in her own mind the same scene he was seeing in his as he thought about it.

It was fun to do, at first, but after Frankie had practiced it on Ilayna and Uriel a few times, she realized that it was hard enough managing her own emotions and the mental images that came into her head, without taking on someone else's as well. She even realized that the more she practiced deliberately sensing other people's thoughts and emotions, the more she felt them, even when she wasn't trying to.

She was glad when Unarius taught her a simple way of blocking out other people's energies. She simply relaxed and envisioned a pillar of white light all around her, keeping out everybody else's thoughts and fears and emotions. Unfortunately, that protective pillar could give way if the thoughts were especially strong. Frankie figured that at home she would have to keep mentally putting that pillar around her over and over again, to block out the thoughts and feelings that people carried around in those dark clouds.

Being invisible was Frankie's favorite lesson, and she practiced it every chance she got until Uriel banned her from the house. Frankie would relax herself, become very still, and then see herself pulling all her energy into her body. Then she would walk quietly up behind Uriel, stand there for a few minutes undetected, and then say, "Boo." Usually Uriel jumped and dropped something. And sometimes it broke. Frankie and Ilayna did that to each other and to Uriel so many times that Uriel finally sent Ilayna off to find herbs and put Frankie to work cleaning the lab.

Frankie's final task was to learn *scrying*. She had heard about scrying in myths and stories about the Greek and Roman gods. In those stories, there always seemed to be somebody who could scry. Usually they called those people oracles or priests or priestesses, because they could see the past and the future, looking across the lines of time and space. There were lots of stories about these *seers*, and often they didn't end well.

Unarius told her that prophesies are not always right, because the future is not really set yet, and it can change as people make different choices—that's where people's free will comes in. Frankie knew that when the oracles and priests were not right, sometimes they got thrown in jail or, worse, burned at the stake. Sometimes when they *were* right they got thrown in jail or burned at the stake, too, because the people thought the seers had caused the problem they foresaw. Even so, Frankie thought it was very exciting, and she wasn't too worried about being punished in Alaris for doing it.

Scrying took a combination of techniques. Frankie had to send her energy out to someone, like she did when she was sensing thoughts and emotions. At the same time, she had to unfocus her eyes and look sideways, like she did when she mentally moved things, and try not to try. She first picked Ilayna as her subject and tried to scry what Ilayna was doing. She sent her energy out to her friend and then unfocused her gaze into Unarius' best crystal ball. It was as big as a ten-pin bowling ball and it was deep and clear, with what looked like a lot of moving and shifting universes deep inside.

Slowly, as she *didn't* concentrate, an image of Ilayna started to form, deep in the center of the ball. And before long Frankie felt like she was there, next to Ilayna in Uriel's lab, mixing and grinding some herbs to make a soothing paste for someone who had come to Uriel with a burned hand. Frankie watched Ilayna add water to the herbs until they formed a thick green paste, and then she patted them onto the man's hand and wrapped it in a clean cotton bandage. Then she did the most important part: She directed healing energy from the palms of her hands toward the injured hand. Uriel had told her that the body used that healing energy to help heal itself. The image disappeared and Frankie "came to" in Unarius' house when Unarius came in, asking her if she was having any luck.

Frankie tried lots of scrying, and soon she decided that she did better if she used a dark bowl full of water. Unarius said that with scrying, and all the other sensings and skills he was teaching her, each person had to find the way that suited her best, because each person does it differently. And most people were better at some types of sensings and ways of working with energy than others.

She discovered her skill with a dark bowl full of water quite by accident one morning at Uriel's house, when she was filling a big dark blue ironstone bowl with water to soak some beans. As she reached for the canister of beans, Frankie was wondering about Aldebaran. She hadn't seen the unicorn for some time and she was missing him and feeling a little neglected. Her heart went out to her magical friend, and she suddenly "saw" his image appear deep in the bowl. He was standing in the workroom with Unarius.

Frankie was so sure that Aldebaran was with Unarius, it was as if he had telephoned and told her so. The image was so clear and strong that she knew it was true. And she had learned to trust that deep knowing instead of doubting herself and talking herself out of it. She jumped up and ran outside, where Uriel and Ilayna were picking tomatoes in the garden.

"Uriel! Ilayna!" she shouted, cupping her hands around her mouth to focus the sound and help it carry out to them, "It's Aldebaran. He's here! He's here! Aldebaran is back!"

11

Clouds of Fear

Frankie wiped her clammy palms against her tunic and then brushed the back of her hand along her hair line to break up the beads of sweat accumulating there as she bounded across the grass toward Unarius' cottage. She was late. She had lingered over breakfast with Ilayna, savoring an extra muffin and a second cup of tea out on the porch. But that was not why she was sweating, not why she was nervous, or even, really, why she was late. Today she had to pass exams.

Today, she was going to demonstrate all of her new skills. Mentally moving objects was a breeze, of course, and she still got a kick out of mentally sending Sebastian back to Uriel's for an unplanned meal once in awhile. Becoming almost invisible was still her favorite thing, if not her best. And she was becoming an old hand at scrying — she still preferred to use a dark bowl full of water to anything else, because that way she could "see" better. She was never quite sure if she was really "seeing" the picture in the bowl or in her head, but it really didn't matter.

The one thing she hadn't really mastered, that she didn't

feel comfortable with, was working with other people's energy fields and thought forms. She could sometimes "read" someone's aura, but Frankie wondered whether she was actually sensing it or merely recognizing the color of the tunic.

The problem was, the whole idea gave her the creeps. She had thought a lot about those dark clouds of anger and fear and pain that could follow people around and infect other people until everyone had their own dark cloud. She wasn't exactly sure she wanted to feel them, so she hadn't really practiced very much. As Frankie ran across the compound, she worried about whether she would be able to demonstrate that for her friends, and her doubts and fears swirled and repeated in her mind over and over again.

As she really got going with that train of thought, Frankie became convinced that she would fail, and then Uriel, Unarius and Aldebaran would all think she was stupid and lazy. Here they had spent so much time and energy trying to help her, but maybe she just couldn't do it. And if she couldn't do it, then she might never be able to get into the fortress in Kelghard and get the key stones back from Janra. And sooner or later Janra and her warriors would find the doorway between worlds and invade her grandfather's house through the portrait on the wall. And it would be all her fault because she just couldn't do anything right. Even her father thought so—he was always getting exasperated and telling her that she was lazy and self-centered and she just didn't try. But she did try. And that made it worse: Even when she tried it seemed she wasn't good enough. . .

Unarius was standing on the porch squinting through a huge quartz crystal at the sky when she arrived, panting.

"I am glad you are here," he said, hardly taking his eyes off the crystal, "but you must get rid of that nasty cloud that you have with you. Do not come in until it is gone." He turned and walked back into the house without another word.

What cloud?

Frankie looked up in the sky and all around, but she could not see what he meant. The bright morning sun had given way to gloomy dark clouds, but that didn't have anything to do with her, did it? She looked down at her tunic and saw it was the color of pond scum. Uh, oh! She retrieved her headband from her pocket, put it on, and suddenly, everything around her looked worse—cold and dead, as if she were standing in the middle of a murky brownish-gray fog. That was because she *was* standing in the middle of a murky brownish-gray fog! She could see the edge of it, and on the other side of that fog was a bright clear sunny day. But she wasn't in that bright day; she was in a day that was dull and brownish gray.

"Oooh-h-h-h-h," she screamed.

The fog took on an angry reddish tinge.

"Stop it!" she shrieked.

It got darker and blacker.

"Leave me alone!" she yelled.

It just got bigger and darker and closed in on her.

"You'll never get rid of it that way." Ilayna called out the door, trying to help. "Focusing your attention on what you do *not* want will only give you *more* of what you do not want. Remember? Focus on what you *want* and *know* that it is here already."

Well, Frankie thought, she wanted it to go away. But it wasn't working. Frankie stared at this hulking black thing that looked like it wanted to devour her and everything around her. This was what Uriel had seen that day when Frankie arrived at the cottage feeling guilty about wanting to stay. And what Unarius had seen when she got angry and frustrated about not being able to move things with her mind. Frankie could see it so clearly now, and it was worse than anything she had imagined when they talked about those thoughtform clouds. This was totally disgusting and gross!

Frankie took the headband off and she could not see it as a limited cloud anymore. But she knew it was still there because everything still looked dull and gray. She could feel it around her, too: chilly, damp, and clammy. And she could see that getting upset about it was only making it worse.

She looked at the bright side: At least this meant that she could not go inside and show everybody that she was a failure! That didn't make her feel any better. She thought a second and realized that she wasn't really a failure, she was just afraid she might be. And being afraid of it and being it were two different things. She hadn't failed. She hadn't even tried yet!

Frankie looked at the dark cloud again. Was it slightly brighter out there? It didn't seem quite as dark as it had been before. She realized she had just as much chance of failing as she did of *not* failing. So maybe she wouldn't? And, she thought, if she was going to have an expectation about her performance, it would be just as easy to expect herself to do well as it is to expect herself to fail. At that thought, the reddish tinge went away.

Unarius had said that the only way to clear up a thoughtform cloud was to consciously recognize her thoughts and emotions. But that was harder than it sounded. She recognized her self-doubt and her fear that she would fail. Feeling those feelings wasn't any fun. What were they trying to tell her? They were telling her that she didn't have any confidence or faith in herself! No wonder she felt awful!

She made herself think about what she had accomplished, instead of what she thought she hadn't learned. She'd mastered just about every skill that Ilayna, Uriel or Unarius had taught her: telekinesis, telepathy, clairvoyance, scrying. These were all things that she couldn't do before, and now she could. And she did them well! As she thought about that, the cloud turned from dark brown to gray.

She clapped.

She thought about how these were things she had never really even heard about, that no one she knew could do them, that people at home just were not taught to do. But she had learned them.

The brown part of the cloud turned sort of beige.

It was working, she thought, and she laughed.

She could clearly see the edges of the cloud now, even without the headband, and as she laughed the cloud got smaller and retreated away from her.

"This is great!" she yelled. Once she recognized her own accomplishments, and gave herself a little credit for them, she felt much better. It was only her fear and self-doubt causing that cloud. "I don't have to be afraid!" she shouted to the sky, shaking her arms and stomping her feet to move that fear energy out of her body. "I'm really smart and I can do all these really neat things! I can do them!" And with that, the dark cloud was gone.

"Unarius!" She jumped up and ran toward the porch, pointing out at the bright, cloudless sunny day. "Uriel, Unarius! Look! It's gone! Look! Aldebaran!"

Unarius, Uriel, Ilayna and Aldebaran came to the doorway, looked out and grinned. "Well of course, my dear," Unarius said. "Very good. Just as expected. Now come inside and you can show off some more for our friends here."

It took her a minute before she realized what he meant. "You mean you expected that to happen?" Frankie asked. "Wait a minute! Was that a test?"

"In a manner of speaking. . . I know you do not feel that you know how to control your thoughtforms," he said, "so I thought I would give you something to work with. I told you about your demonstration, knowing you would feel it was a test that you must pass or fail, and knowing you would likely worry and doubt yourself into a dark cloud about it. Which you did. And then you saw it, you recognized your thoughts and feelings, and you changed them. End of the so-called test. Now that you really understand what can happen, perhaps you will stop believing all those negative things about yourself and letting your thoughts run wild. Because every time you concentrate on those negative thoughts, you make yourself feel bad and create a cloud just like that. You actually poison yourself with those bad thoughts when you do that." He turned and walked back into the cottage. "Next time you have those doubts about yourself, I want you to remember this little exercise, and realize that you can do whatever you set your mind to. The hardest part seems to be getting you to believe it!"

Frankie bounded into the cottage and threw her arms around the unicorn's neck. "Oh Aldebaran, it's been so long! And I saw you coming, you know. I saw you in Uriel's favorite stoneware bowl!"

"I know you did, Frankie, I could feel your energy reaching out to me."

"You could?"

"Of course, I could. You're not the only one who can feel someone else's energy, you know." He leaned against her and invited her to pet his silky mane.

"But where have you been, Aldebaran? Why did you leave for so long?"

The unicorn snorted and nudged her on the rear end with his nose, gently pushing her toward the workroom. "Believe it or not, I have other things to do besides watch you learn your lessons. If you will notice, however, I returned when it was time to put them to use. Are you ready to go to Kelghard?"

Frankie didn't answer. She couldn't, because there was suddenly a lump the size of her fist right in the middle of her throat. She stopped in her tracks and became very interested in the unicorn's mane again. She ran her fingers through it, picked up a few strands and idly braided it, and generally tried not to notice that her tunic was turning muddy purple.

"Frankie has done very well and mastered all of her lessons, even if she does not quite believe it herself," Unarius told the unicorn, patting her comfortingly on the shoulder and starting the progression back toward the workroom again. "But I think she is becoming a bit nervous at the idea of the *next steps*."

"I should hope so," said Aldebaran. "If Frankie were not nervous, I would be worried. She is not going on a picnic, she is going to be doing something very important that could be dangerous. And she needs to take it seriously."

By this time, thick brownish-black smoke was rising up around Frankie's head.

"I am sorry, Frankie," he said, resting his chin on her arm, "but we would not be doing you a favor if we pretended this endeavor may not have elements of difficulty or danger."

"I know," she answered, petting his mane again because it seemed like the one thing that could give her comfort, "but suddenly, I'm very scared."

"And what have you learned about fear?"

"It helps you by pointing out things you need to look at or pay attention to," Frankie answered, remembering what Unarius had told her. She noticed that Unarius nodded and smiled at her. She tried to smile back.

"That is correct," Aldebaran said, lifting his head to look straight into her eyes. "And your fear is warning you that there might be danger. So you heed that warning. You do not let it stop you, you let it teach you. You train yourself so you will be as well prepared as you can be to do what you have decided you must do." He went to the other end of the work room to give her some space to work in. "And now, Frankie, I have been told that you have trained very hard and learned many new skills, and I want to see a demonstration."

At first, Frankie was nervous that she would make a mistake or do something dumb. But she closed her eyes and took three very deep slow breaths, breathing in with her nose, then breathing out even slower through her mouth, the way Unarius had shown her. He said this would relax her and help her to feel more balanced and supported. Whatever it did, it worked, and her doubts and fears ebbed away.

She asked Unarius to get a bowl of water for scrying, and while he was gone Frankie showed off some of her new skills for Uriel and Aldebaran. She mentally summoned Sebastian, who jumped up from his sunny spot on the porch, came bounding into the room, slid across the floor, and screeched to a halt at her feet, licking his chops. She got him some catnip from a bag on the counter to make his trip worthwhile.

Unarius came back with the bowl of water, set it down on a side counter, leaned against the door jamb, and watched.

Frankie gathered up her energy, focused it, and mentally asked the water-filled bowl to float across the room to the table next to Aldebaran, supporting it with her own energy as it moved, without a drop being spilled. After that, just for the fun of it, she sent the dozen or so daffodils on the desk flying out of their vase in all directions, then gathered them up and put them back—all without touching them.

She was not sure how to demonstrate her telepathy until she nudged Unarius and then Uriel with her energy and picked up the same thought. "Okay, you two," she said, "I've discovered your secret! You guys are having a party for me, aren't you? Ilayna's doing the decorating right now!"

Unarius blushed, coughed, scuffed his foot, and generally assured her that she was right without ever saying a word. Uriel applauded and laughed.

"That sounds very festive, Frankie," Aldebaran said, "but you will have to wait until your 'graduation exercises' are concluded! I have not seen you scry yet."

Frankie retrieved the bowl from the table. She closed her eyes and told her body to relax as she did her three deep breaths again. She opened her eyes, unfocused them and looked sideways at the bowl. An image slowly began to appear of lots of people, people dressed like Janra's warriors. They were laughing and drinking. Over their shoulders she could see other warriors on horses riding toward each other. As she went deeper into the vision, she could almost hear the cheers of the crowd as one warrior fell to the ground and the other rode past him in triumph. She could smell the sweat of the horses mingled with the smell of soft warm hay. She pulled herself back and looked at the unicorn.

"It looks like they're jousting," she said. "I see a festival of some kind in Kelghard. Everyone is there. But I get the feeling that it hasn't happened yet. It's going to happen."

Aldebaran pranced over to her side. "That is excellent, Frankie. Not only did you see something important, but you also reminded me of what I had to tell you, if I thought you were ready. And I think you *are* ready. It will be best if we leave here in the morning. Janra is having a jousting tournament for her warriors the following day, and that will be a good time for you to go into the fortress at Kelghard and retrieve the key stones, when most of the people will be outside at the fairgrounds. It will be the safest time to go."

Before Aldebaran finished speaking, Frankie dropped the bowl and it splintered into tiny pieces at her feet.

12

Many Voices Weigh In

Frankie and Aldebaran left the next morning. In a way, Frankie was glad that it happened so fast, because she didn't have time to sit around worrying about it. She knew that she had learned as much as she could. She also knew that she couldn't afford to waste time. While she dallied and quibbled, Janra might make the first move. And Frankie wouldn't be able to find the key stones if she were in a cell in the Kelghard fortress dungeon.

Ilayna's mother had sent word that Janra had people watching them, so Ilayna, Uriel and Unarius planned to join Frankie and Aldebaran later in the forest not far from Kelghard. Four people and a unicorn traveling toward Kelghard might arouse suspicion, especially these four people.

As they reached the other side of Alaris and started to climb the terraced steps up into the hills, the feel of the warm sun on her arms reminded Frankie of her last trip along this road. The weather had been spectacular then, too. She had started on a big adventure that day, and here she was, starting out on another one. Last time, she had been confused but excited. This time, she was afraid.

"Why do I have to do this, Aldebaran?" she suddenly asked, lowering her voice as if ashamed to be overheard. She felt guilty, somehow, because she was afraid and because she did not want to have to do this alone. She was even more afraid that she wouldn't be able to do what she needed to do.

"Frankie, I have told you, you do not have to do this," he answered, as she knew he would. "You feel that you *must* do this because you believe it must be done—and no one else is volunteering."

"*Someone* has to!" Frankie retorted, making his point. "But why can't it be someone else? I'm just a kid! I shouldn't have to do this."

"You want someone to come and fix it for you, is that it?"

"That would be nice. I guess." She kicked a rock out of her way but didn't say anything else.

"You do not need to feel guilty about wanting someone else to come and fix it. Everyone wants that to happen, especially when they are facing something that is frightening and might be difficult or dangerous," Aldebaran said softly, "or if they feel ill-equipped for the task. That usually does not happen, no matter what the story books say. But if you always have other people rescuing you and fixing your life, then you will really begin to believe that you *cannot* do it yourself. You always feel better about yourself when you know you *can* do it, when you face your challenges yourself and succeed."

"You mean I always have to do it myself, with no help?"

"No, my friend, that is not what I said," Aldebaran said, giving her a nudge with his nose, sending her skipping ahead of him, giggling. "You may have to fight your own battles, but you always will have available to you the help that you need. You may have to ask for that help, and you may not recognize it for what it is when it arrives, because it does not come in the form you expect, but help is *always* available."

Frankie knew that he was right, but that didn't make it any

easier. She still had to go into Kelghard fortress, find the key stones, find the crystal with the missing part of her Aunt Cassandra, and get them—and herself—out. Even with the help she'd had getting ready to go, Frankie wasn't sure how she could do all that by herself.

As she wrinkled her brow in confusion, Aldebaran gave a funny throaty snort that was the closest he ever got to laughing. "I can almost see the voices arguing about it in your head, my friend!"

Frankie laughed. That was exactly what was happening, and she told him so. It wasn't like voices from outside or from other people, but she definitely had lots of different voices arguing with each other in her head. One of the voices said, *Go ahead, you can do it*; another said, *Are you crazy??* One said, *Be careful*, and another said, *Don't worry*. And one screamed very loudly that she would get caught, get thrown in the dungeon, and be lost forever! Frankie stooped down, picked up a small round rock and aimed it at a tree six or seven yards away. She threw it and hit the trunk squarely.

"How am I supposed to decide what to do, with all that racket in my head?" she clapped her hands over her ears and winced. "How am I supposed to know which one to listen to? How can I get them all to just shut up?"

Aldebaran snorted again. "Yes, it can be very distracting. Do not worry; you are not the only one who experiences this interesting human phenomenon. Everyone has many voices inside, Frankie, and you merely have to learn which voice is which. They are just the voices of your thoughts and emotions. They want your attention; they want to be heard. After you have listened to them, they will be quiet and you can decide what to do. It can feel that you are being beset by harpies, but they are really more like your own private set of advisors."

It was a relief to know that she was not the only one who had these mental arguments. She had started to think she must be crazy. She also thought it would be nice to know who all these different voices were.

"But who do they belong to," she asked, "and why won't they be quiet? Sometimes they get so loud I can't think!"

Aldebaran brought his nose right up to her cheek and breathed softly. His breath was warm and soft and smelled like wild flowers. Then he rubbed his nose against hers. To Frankie, it felt like a unicorn kiss, the sweetest thing she could imagine.

"They are all your own voices, Frankie—from different parts of you," he said. "And they each have a specific job to do for you. Sometimes they all agree on what you should do, and then you feel very sure of what you are doing, and it happens easily. That is called total alignment or being in the flow. It is like being in a small boat and the tide carries you in the direction you want to go, without the effort of rowing.

"But most of the time," he added, "the many parts of you disagree and they argue, each one clamoring for your attention. Then it is more like you are rowing in circles or, worse, rowing against the tide."

"Is that what people mean when they say they're of two minds about something?" Frankie asked, thinking it was more like being of twenty or thirty minds.

Aldebaran nodded. "Yes. And often they say they have warring emotions, which, in fact, they do."

Frankie nodded, too, and shifted her backpack a bit. They had been walking for an hour or so, and she hoped they would stop for lunch soon. She was starting to wish she was traveling with Uriel, Unarius, and Ilayna. They would be using a small horse and cart, borrowed from Ilayna's mother.

They walked along in silence for a while, caught up in their own thoughts.

"Perhaps I can help you understand some of those voices in your head," Aldebaran said after some time. "One voice is concerned with keeping you safe. It can be very handy to have around, because it reminds you to take care of yourself and it can make you aware of possible danger. But sometimes, it can hold you back, because it would rather have you sit at home and do nothing than take the risk of being hurt in any way. That voice is like an overprotective parent. It thinks life is dangerous."

He paused and thought a moment before he went on, and Frankie could almost feel his mind, like gentle fingers, touching hers. "Another voice is the part of you that is afraid of failure. You have that voice because someone taught you when you were young that you must be perfect and not take risks or make mistakes. It urges you not to try new things because you might not succeed, and it clings to its comfortable routines and hates any kind of change."

Frankie knew which one he meant. That voice played the "what if" game in her head, bringing up all the things that could go wrong, all the ways she could fail or look silly. That voice didn't care that she might be hurt, it only cared that she might fail. When she listened to that voice, she stopped herself from trying new things.

"Another voice wants fun and adventure and is quite happy to let the other parts worry about danger or risk. That voice knows you are safe and protected in the Universe. Are these some of the voices you hear?"

Frankie nodded, "Yes. And I can name another one. One that's not very nice."

"Tell me about that one," Aldebaran said.

She did. This voice criticized her and everything she did. It told her she was lazy, stupid, ugly, and unlovable. It made her feel self-conscious and awkward, and sometimes she even started to believe all the bad things it said about her. And sometimes, although she hated to admit it, she thought it sounded like her Dad.

"That mental voice is your Critic," Aldebaran said. "Almost everyone has that and it is a nasty one. It hears all the bad, mean things that other people have said to you—and any mean things that *you* have said—and it plays them back to you over and over again. And most people come to believe it. The way to get that voice to be quiet is to let it know that you hear what it says, but you know it is wrong and you do not believe what it tells you. The Critic voice does not know it is wrong. It is trying to be helpful by repeating what it has heard. You must believe in yourself and not pay so much attention to the voice of criticism, whether it comes from inside your head or from someone else."

Frankie sighed. That was easy for a unicorn to say! But she was glad when he reminded her that one of those voices in her head was the voice of Source, the voice of calm and peace that loved and accepted her just the way she was. That was the one she needed to learn to recognize and to listen to more! And Aldebaran said that voice, that presence, is always available, she just has to ask and listen.

When the sun was straight up above them, they stopped and ate lunch at a shaded spot by a cool spring. While Frankie munched on tomato and cheese sandwiches, made with Uriel's homemade bread, Aldebaran snacked on the fragrant green grass. After they ate, Frankie splashed cold water from the spring onto her face and then jumped up, laughing, and squirted water at Aldebaran. He retaliated by dropping a bunch of grass on her head. Their laughter, human and unicorn, echoed around them as they started on their way again.

Even though it was a long walk, it was easy terrain, and Frankie found that talking to Aldebaran made the time pass quickly. She also noticed that when she started to tire, she could feel him sending her energy. Every once in awhile Frankie would laugh out loud at the very idea that she was walking through the mountains with a unicorn and it all felt perfectly normal! No one at home would ever believe her!

It wasn't long before they reached the place where they would meet the others and camp for the night. Aldebaran led her through a field of high grass toward a thick part of the forest. They followed a concealed path deep into the trees, and finally came into a large clearing filled with grass and flowers, encircled by tall redwood trees. It was like a magic place where one could hide and never be found, and Frankie wouldn't have been surprised to see sprites and fairies and magical beings dancing around the huge fire pit in the center of the clearing. Instead, she had to make do with a small beige fawn and a family of gray rabbits who came over to greet them. Frankie felt a little left out because it was clear that the unicorn and the animals spoke a language that she didn't know.

Frankie had gathered a pile of kindling and was resting on one of the great logs placed around the fire pit, trying to make friends with a rabbit, when Uriel, Unarius and Ilayna arrived, calling to her and laughing as they entered the clearing. Frankie was glad to see them, and her spirits rose as she joined in with their unpacking.

It didn't take very long to get the camp set up and looking like they had been there for weeks. Uriel helped Frankie get the rest of the wood they would need for the fire, Ilayna toted water in large canvas containers from the stream, and Unarius unpacked the supplies and put things out on a large green blanket. There was lots of delicious-looking food, and Frankie realized that she was both hungry and tired from her journey. As the sun started to disappear into a faint orange glow over the trees, they lit the fire, rolled out their bedrolls, and sat down on the logs to eat dinner.

By the time they finished eating, the stars were out. There was no lingering twilight in Alaris and here, more than at home, Frankie understood the idea that night falls. There were thousands of stars, bright and pulsing against the inky sky, and the full moon seemed to smile down at them. The Man in the Moon looked to be at home and happy. Crickets and tree toads said good night to each other and the fire glowed warm and comforting. In dreamy voices they talked quietly about Alaris and Kelghard, about Cassandra and Cybele and the Wise Ones, and about Aradia's dreams of uniting all the people in peace and her sister Janra's dreams of conquest.

It was not long, though, before they all sought out their beds. Although the unicorn never seemed tired, he settled down next to Frankie so that when she put her hand out to the side, she could feel his soft mane. She caught a few silky strands in her fingers and held them lightly as she fell asleep, the voices in her head finally quiet.

13

A Warrior's Send-off

Frankie felt as if she had barely closed her eyes when the birds and forest animals loudly announced the dawn. She could hear her friends beginning to move about the clearing, but she lay still for a few more minutes, savoring the comforting sounds and the feeling of being safely surrounded by people who loved her. Plenty of time to get up and face what Frankie figured would be the most challenging day of her life.

Like a movie running across her mind, Frankie reviewed all that she had experienced and learned since she had stumbled through the portrait in her grandparents' house and landed with a thud on the floor of the cottage in Alaris. It had been a grand adventure, and Frankie was grateful that she had found such loving, wise friends who had taught her so much, mostly about herself. If things went wrong today, Frankie knew—if she were captured by Janra again—she might never escape or see her friends again. If things went *right* today—if she found everything she was looking for in Kelghard and managed to get back to the cottage in the clearing, to that door between worlds—she would go through that door. . . and she might never see these dear friends again. Either way, she would lose them, and she felt an ache in her chest as she thought about that.

This time, only a couple of the voices in her head called out for her attention. One voice spoke of her deep sadness at having to leave these wonderful people—and one magical, grumpy unicorn—who had come to mean so much to her. But another voice pointed out that she was doing what she had to do—doing what she came here to do. Frankie recognized deep down inside that this was her path to walk, and for once, she could agree with all those voices in her head.

The clearing felt charged with the energy of sadness, hope, and anticipation as they prepared and ate their breakfast.

After breakfast, Uriel drew them over to the fire pit, telling Frankie that they would send her off on her quest as the warrior that she had become. Uriel had placed a large quartz crystal on each of four large stones around the fire, marking north, east, south, and west, and they all stood around the circle. Unarius struck a chime and the haunting note lingered in the air. Ilayna threw spices onto the burning embers, and the scent of cinnamon and cloves wafted up. Then Uriel passed around a cup filled with mead for each person to drink from, in turn. To Frankie, it smelled of honey and wildflowers. Then came little carrot cakes, one for each. These things represented the four elements, Uriel said: air, water, fire, and earth. Then they joined hands and danced, clockwise, around the fire. Unarius, Uriel and Ilayna sang a song of strength and courage, and Aldebaran pranced and whinnied along with them. Frankie could only hum because she didn't know the words. But she felt the music reaching deep down inside her, making her feel strong and capable.

Then each of them hugged Frankie, whispered their own private message in her ear, and gave her a token for her journey. Ilayna gave her a hand-made silver bracelet with a garnet in the middle; the garnet was supposed to bring success and a safe journey and was said to change color when evil approached. Unarius gave her a pair of amethyst earrings; the amethysts would raise her energy and bring success and calmness in danger. And Uriel gave her a necklace made with turquoise and dark blue lapis lazuli, for courage, confidence, and protection.

At the end, Aldebaran told her to put her hand on his horn, something that she had always wanted to do, but had never dared. As she slowly wrapped her hand around his golden horn, she could feel warmth and courage and determination flowing straight up her arm and down her body to her toes. When she let go, she knew deep inside that, somehow, the magic of the unicorn would always be with her and she really could face anything.

But there was one thing she did not want to have to face.

"I won't actually have to fight with Janra, will I?" she asked, almost afraid to hear the answer. Unlike her Aunt Cassie, who had fiercely fought Belzar, Frankie knew she would be a sorry match for Janra.

"By no means, child!" Uriel exclaimed, holding her in a great bear hug. "Janra is a warrior. You are a young girl. You must be what you are and do what you do. Now and always. That is what is needed here. That is what is always needed." Uriel held Frankie at arm's length and looked her in the eye to be sure she understood. "You must never try to be what you are *not*, because it *always* goes wrong if you do. If a warrior were needed now, we would have a warrior here. Obviously, what is needed for this situation is a young girl. And not just any young girl: YOU! So here you are! Remember this, Frankie: You will always succeed if you stay true to yourself."

Frankie breathed a sigh of relief at that, feeling that she had a much better chance of being herself than she did of being a warrior. And, being a young girl, she was hoping to sneak into that fortress, retrieve the stones, and retreat without Janra ever knowing she was there. That was her plan, anyway.

As she gathered her backpack to go, she watched Aldebaran conferring with Uriel and Unarius. She could just barely see him flicker every once in awhile as they talked. It wasn't the first time that Frankie wondered if Aldebaran was the unicorn that Aunt Cassie had ridden in that battle with Belzar. The unicorn she'd seen in her dream had been huge and fierce, while Aldebaran was much smaller. But Frankie had always felt that Aldebaran adjusted his size for her, so she wouldn't be afraid. Either way, she couldn't imagine anyone — even Aunt Cassie with spears and swords — having the nerve, or being given permission, to ride on the back of a unicorn! Particularly this one! But still. . . she wondered.

Frankie was glad that they would take the horse and cart when they left for Kelghard, so she wouldn't be tired when they arrived.

And she was glad that Ilayna was coming with her. Ilayna was able to come and go at the fortress, visiting her mother when she pleased. They hoped that Ilayna's presence would smooth the way for Frankie to get past the guards at the gate, without raising too many questions. If necessary, Ilayna could also act as a diversion. Frankie was just glad she was coming.

As they headed out toward the fortress, with Ilayna managing the horse and Aldebaran walking alongside the cart, Frankie had a clear view of the road ahead. It seemed strange that this dusty road to Kelghard, on this parallel world, would be an important part of her road in life. Parts of her wished she would suddenly realize that it was all a mistake, that this was the wrong road after all. *Never mind! Just a detour! My mistake!* But she knew it wasn't a mistake. She sighed.

"Are you worried about what will happen, Frankie?" Ilayna asked.

"I'm worried, all right," Frankie said, "but I was really wondering why this is my road to travel. Who decided that, anyway?"

"Well, it's really the fastest way to Kelghard," Ilayna said. "If you don't take this road, you have to go through the forest."

"I do not think she means the direction we are going or the actual road, Ilayna," he said. "Do you, Frankie?"

"No," she answered, "it's this road of life thing you talked about."

"That's a deep question that most humans do not ask," he said as they made their way along the wide track. "You see, every human has a road to follow in life, a path to take, a role to play. It is why you are here. You mapped out your road ahead of time, before you were born. You decided that in this life you wanted to learn this or that, do something or other. You may have even agreed to meet different people, to marry one, introduce someone to somebody else, be best friends or worst enemies with others. When you meet these people, you have a feeling that you have met them before or that you have known them all your life. Deep inside, a part of you recognizes them; a part of you says, 'ah, *there* you are.'"

Frankie and Ilayna grinned at each other, liking the idea that they had somehow arranged ahead of time to meet each other, even living in different worlds. Frankie had had that feeling with other people, too. "But how do you know what you're supposed to do and where your road is or where it leads?" she asked. "I don't remember any map or plan."

"There lies the difficulty," Aldebaran said. "That is why poets and philosophers down through Time have talked about finding their *purpose in life*. Unfortunately, many become so caught up in trying to figure it out with their heads that they do not listen to their hearts or the deep inner part of them that actually *remembers* what their purpose is! Humans are so very funny, they always make things so complicated!"

"Funny to you, maybe," Frankie said. "Do you mean that inner sense that Uriel talked about?"

"Exactly," he said, with a little whinny. "There is a special part in each person, deep inside, that is still connected to All There Is, to Source, to everything in the universe. That part of you remembers Who You Are and it remembers the road you mapped out for yourself. People call it different things: the soul, the spirit, the higher self, or the inner self. The name does not matter. That is the part that nudges and prompts you along and keeps you going where you want to go, even when you do not remember you want to go there. You can tell you are listening to that inner part when you follow your intuition, pay attention to your gut reactions, and do the things that make you feel happy and interested and good about yourself. When you feel deeply unhappy and uncomfortable, that is a sure sign that you are on the wrong road."

Frankie laughed. Aldebaran always made things sound so easy! She might be on her road, but she was not feeling particularly happy or good about it. Besides, why would she give herself a road this hard and dangerous?

"Remember, Frankie," the unicorn said as if he had read her mind, "you would not give yourself a road that you could not follow. Would you feel good about yourself if you stopped right now and did not try to get the crystal key stones back from Janra? If you just left that part of your Aunt Cassie frozen through Time in a crystal? If you just stopped and went back to Alaris to play and have fun?"

Frankie thought about it for a minute, trying to be as honest as she could be with herself. One voice in her head screamed "YES!", but at the same time the muscles in her shoulders got tense and scrunched up and hard, and her head started to throb over her left eye. Every doubt was gone in that one minute. She was afraid to go—that was true enough. But she would feel terrible about herself if she didn't try. She just felt that she had to do this, no matter how scary it was. No matter what!

Aldebaran waited until he could see her shoulders relax, knowing that meant she had found her answer. Then he continued. "Everyone's road is different, and everyone's road has easy parts and rough parts. Sometimes the road spreads out before you, wide and clear and sure." He nodded at the road ahead of them and Frankie could almost feel him smile.

"Well, this *looks* easy, but I'm not so sure!" she said.

"It is true that looks can be deceiving," he said. "Other times the road is narrow, with rocks and holes and detours. Or you might run into heavy fog so you can see only one step in front of you at a time, and you have to feel your way along. But no matter how hard the road looks, you must always believe—you must always *know* deep inside—that you *will* be able to travel it. Do not let your fear stop you from trying."

"I'm lucky that my road is so clear," Ilayna said, "I've always known I would be a healer, like Uriel."

Aldebaran snorted. "You are lucky that this *part* of your road is clear and easy, Ilayna," he said, "but you know it has not always been so, nor will it always be so."

Ilayna looked so distressed that Frankie laughed. "At least we're on the road together now, Ilayna," she said. "And if I have to travel this road, I'm glad you and Aldebaran are here with me."

"The traveling is always easier when you find someone to share it with," Aldebaran agreed. "But sometimes people can only share your road for a time, and when you come to a turn you must take, they may not like it. They might try to convince you that you are taking the wrong road or that you should stay on their road instead. A side trip now and then can be refreshing, but if you venture off your road and stay too long, then you will not feel very good about yourself. You will start to feel depressed and unhappy, and you will know that something is very wrong. You will not feel right again until you find your way back to the right road for you."

Frankie nodded, thinking about one of her uncles. "It's like if your parents want you to be a doctor, but you want to be a teacher, right? If you become a doctor just to please them, you're on *their* road. If you become a teacher, you're on your road—but they might say you made the wrong choice!"

"Precisely!" Aldebaran agreed, as if that solved the problem. "And often they have what seem to be very good reasons for saying you have made the wrong choice: You will not make as much money, or everyone is *supposed* to do the other thing. But they will be wrong. Now, sometimes, it is very good if you can compromise—become a doctor and then teach others to be doctors—but that is not always possible. Each time, you have to make a choice. And sometimes that can be very hard, especially if you do not trust yourself and if you are worried about being liked and making other people, rather than yourself, happy."

Frankie knew what he meant. She was already running into situations at school that were forcing her to make hard choices. New friends wanted her to drop her old friends and everyone was feeling the pressure to be popular, to be cool—to decide what is cool and what you are willing to do to be cool and popular. Frankie knew that as she got older and started dating the decisions would only become harder and more complicated. She looked at Ilayna and thought it didn't seem so hard in Alaris.

"It's not always easy, is it?" she asked with a sigh.

"No, it is by no means always easy," Aldebaran agreed. "But if you calm yourself and ask the question, with an open heart and an open mind, the answer will come to you. And each time you make a choice to stay on your own road, to be true to who you are and what you believe in, then each time it gets easier. But no, my friend, it is not always easy. Not for anyone."

Frankie chewed on that for awhile, as they traveled along, and all too soon she realized that the road had been filling up with other travelers heading toward Kelghard. When they rounded a wide curve in the road, Frankie was stunned to realize that they had actually reached their destination. Her stomach suddenly seemed to fill up with bees as she eyed the fortress and tried not to think about what was going to happen next.

Carefully steering the horse and cart, Ilayna threaded her way through the other travelers and off the road into the meadow until she found a convenient place at the edge of the forest for them to rest and regroup. Ilayna unhitched the horse and he nibbled on the fragrant grass while Ilayna, Frankie, and Aldebaran discussed strategy and consulted the map of the fortress that Ilayna's mother, Aradia, had given them.

Fortunately, Kelghard didn't have a moat, but there was an expanse of open meadow stretching about the length of a football field from the edge of the forest to the fortress, which was perched on a wide, flat plateau on a hill. Frankie wasn't worried about riding up to the fortress in the cart with Ilayna, but she knew she might have to cross that open area by herself on the way out.

"This is the outer bailey," Ilayna said, pointing to the outer wall on the map. It held round towers at intervals, and the entire wall was topped with battlements, where guards would be stationed. The gatehouse at the main entrance had a tower on either side.

"We'll go through the gatehouse at the top of the hill," Ilayna said. "There will be guards questioning people as they get close to the entrance, but I think I will be able to get us past them without any trouble. Most of the guards know me."

Frankie felt the hair stand up on the back of her neck as

she thought about trying to get past all the guards stationed at the giant main doors and up on the battlements.

"Then we'll cross the open area and on into the main courtyard. That's where we'll find the stables and leave the horse and cart," Ilayna continued, tracing the way with her finger on the map. "Jaimie works in the stables, and he likes me. So I think he'll hold the cart ready for us."

Frankie's vision seemed to fade in and out for a minute, as it all started to feel entirely too real.

"The tournament will be set up in the fields behind the keep. That's over here, to the right," Ilayna said. "See the round towers at the corners? We'll go in there to avoid crossing the great hall. . ."

Frankie shuddered as she looked at those towers. Those awful men had dragged her into the keep through a door in one of those towers the last time she was here. She shuddered again just thinking about it.

The ground floor of the great hall held large public rooms, and the second floor housed the sleeping quarters. Ilayna pointed out the location of Janra's rooms on the second floor. The storeroom, where she hoped to find the crystal key stones, was in the same section, but one floor below ground.

"Wouldn't you know they'd put it in the basement?" Frankie said, jabbing the paper with her finger. "I hate basements; they can be so damp and creepy!" Even worse, Janra's dungeons were down there. Frankie had marked the dungeons in red pencil on the map—this was an area that she planned to avoid at all costs!

Once Frankie had a good idea where she needed to go, she carefully folded the map and put it in her pocket.

The plan was that Ilayna and Frankie would enter the fortress and retrieve the pink heart-shaped key stone and the six-sided quartz crystal key stone. They would also look for the crystal cluster that held that small part of Aunt Cassie, the crystal that held Cybele, and any others that looked important and would fit into Frankie's backpack. Then they would return to this spot, meet Aldebaran, and return with him to the clearing in the forest, where Frankie would say her good-byes and go back through the portal, locking the portal closed behind her.

They even had contingency plans. If Ilayna and Frankie got separated, Frankie would do what she could by herself and meet Ilayna at the stables so they could collect the horse and cart. If Ilayna wasn't there, Frankie would leave without her.

If Frankie couldn't meet Aldebaran on the way back for some reason, or if she was pursued, she was to keep going along this path for about 10 minutes and bear right at the great oak, onto an overgrown path that Aldebaran had carefully pointed out. If she could follow it, it was the fastest route, through the thickest part of the forest, to the cottage.

If all else failed, she might be able to make it back to her own world with at least one of the key stones, and lock the door behind her. That was assuming she was able to find the key stones and get out without being caught.

They all knew they were dealing with a lot of "ifs": if she could find the key stones, if she could get out without being caught, if she could get back to the cottage and get through the portal. But Frankie knew that all she could do was try her best—and there were no "ifs" about that!

With their plans in place, it was time to go. While Ilayna hitched up the horse, Aldebaran gently offered Frankie what strength he could and then flickered and blurred out of sight, letting her see him briefly in his larger, fiercer guise before he vanished completely. To the very last, Frankie saw a single, golden tear running down the side of his silvery white face.

It was her road to go to the fortress, she reminded herself. Her friends had helped her as much as they could and now it was up to her. Aldebaran's road, he said, was to have to stand back and let her go, knowing that he couldn't help. Frankie thought his might be the harder road. Even if she was afraid she might fail, it seemed easier to at least be able to try to do something than to have to stand by and watch without being able to help.

With that thought, Frankie took a deep breath, put on a long cloak that would cover her jeans and sweater, checked to see that her crystal headband was settled firmly across her forehead, and she and Ilayna headed out toward Kelghard Fortress and her destiny.

14

Into the Fortress

As the cart slowly made its way toward the gatehouse, caught up in the snarl of people trying to get in, Frankie caught a glimpse of the tournament field on the far side of the fortress. There were grandstands and tents set up, with colorful banners flying in the breeze. The breeze also carried the scent of roasting beef as cooks prepared food for the throngs, and Frankie's stomach rumbled as the tantalizing smell reached her nose. People hustled about, setting out items for sale and putting the finishing touches on the decorations, and crowds of people were heading toward the field from every direction.

The tournament was already in progress and, under her breath, Ilayna pointed out that there were only a few guards up on the ramparts, and they were paying more attention to the tournament field than anything else. The guards by the gatehouse were the only ones who were paying attention to the people swarming in. As they moved past them, the guards were so busy smiling and nodding to Ilayna that they barely noticed Frankie sitting in the cart beside her.

Ilayna maneuvered the cart away from the crowds and

across the wide courtyard toward the stables. Fortunately, the courtyard was fairly empty except for a few stragglers who were hurrying out toward the tournament field. As they reached the stables, a boy of about 10, covered in dirt to his elbows, ducked in a quick bow to Ilayna and started removing the horse's harness.

"Oh, no, Jamie," Ilayna stopped him. "We won't be very long, so I want you to keep Daisy hitched to the cart."

"That Daisy won't be liking that none, ma'am," he said, his big blue eyes glowing bright in his grimy face.

"I know she won't, Jamie," Ilayna said, "but maybe you could feed her a few carrots and give her a good brushing to make her feel better while she waits."

He brightened, reaching into a deep pocket in his tunic and bringing out a carrot. "She'd like that well enough, I 'spect. I al'ays has a carrot for my Daisy."

"I know you do, Jamie," Ilayna said as she steered Frankie toward a round tower in the corner. "We should be back soon. If my friend comes out without me, you can let her take Daisy and the cart by herself. All right?"

"Yessum, Miss 'Layna," he said as Daisy made a grab for the carrot in his hand, "I'll have it ready right here."

Frankie pulled her cloak closer around her to cover her jeans and sweater. Then she checked to make sure the hood was covering her head and hiding her crystal headband. Even so, she felt like her white sneakers stuck out like a sore thumb. She could imagine big red neon arrows hanging in the air above, pointing at them. She knew, though, that if she kept focusing on feeling conspicuous and vulnerable, then surely she would attract unwanted attention. So she took three deep breaths, and relaxed her shoulders. Then, for safe measure, she slowly pulled in her energy to make herself as invisible as possible.

"We must go before someone comes," Ilayna said into her

ear, as she took her arm and steered her toward the tower door. They had almost reached the doorway when Ilayna suddenly stepped away, turning her back to Frankie. Frankie turned to see what was happening, then quickly turned away again as she saw Ilayna greet a tall man wearing Janra's colors coming out of the stables.

"Miss Ilayna," he said, with a brief nod, "I don't believe we were expecting you at the tournament today." He sounded displeased.

"I hadn't planned to come, Darius," she said, "but I couldn't resist. I was just going to meet my mother in her chamber." As she talked to the guard, Ilayna's hand motioned furiously behind her back, urging Frankie to keep walking through the door.

But Frankie was already on her way. She pulled in her energy again, just to be sure, and walked in a measured pace toward the door. As she walked over the threshold, her heart sank as she heard the guard's reply: "Princess Aradia is out at the lists already, Miss. I will take you there myself." He offered Ilayna his arm, but he made it sound like an order.

No! No! NO! The voices in Frankie's head started to shriek. But Frankie knew that Ilayna had no choice but to go with Darius. Now Frankie was really on her own!

Frankie stood a moment on the landing just inside the door, trying to get her bearings and build up her nerve. Since she didn't hear anyone coming on the steps, she pulled out the map and reoriented herself. The tower stairway was in one corner of the building. One flight up would take her to the residence wing, where Janra's rooms were located. One flight down would take her to the storage and work rooms. Two flights down—she shuddered when she thought of it—would take her to the dungeons. She would avoid that floor at all costs!

Frankie started down the narrow stone spiral stairs toward

the storage rooms, putting off going to Janra's rooms again as long as possible. When she reached the door at the landing one flight down, she listened, then pushed the door open a crack and peered out. No one was in sight. She mentally pulled in her energy again and envisioned a column of light around herself to keep it that way. Spreading out before her was a long stone hallway with a number of heavy doors on each side. All was quiet, so she tip-toed into the hallway. These doors must lead to the storerooms. Unfortunately, she might have to look in all of them. Too bad they didn't have signs posted for her convenience!

Feeling rather bold, she walked faster down the hallway and peered into the first room on her right. She stopped inside the door and gasped. Her heart started pounding and she could feel the blood rush up into her head. She had practically walked right into a man. A silver man. A man in full armor. He must be on his way out to the tournament, Frankie thought with alarm. He should have been out there already. The man didn't move and neither did she.

Frankie just stood there, staring at his silver visor. She felt like her heart would explode. Why didn't he do something?

She studied the metal helm and the body armor. She looked lower and suddenly realized there wasn't a man inside after all. It was an old discarded suit of armor. She relaxed, looked around the room, and gasped again at what she saw.

The room was filled with all kinds of old armor and weapons. Rows and rows and racks and racks and piles and piles of them, all over the room. Frankie knew about old pieces of armor and weapons, the pikes and maces and flails and crossbows, from lessons and books about the crusades, and from the television shows and stories about Robin Hood. Did Janra's warriors use these things? Frankie shuddered. If they caught her, they might use one of these hideous weapons on her. Or worse.

She shook herself to clear the thought out of her head. To dwell on something was to bring it to you. Better to think about what she wanted. She mentally pictured herself holding the pink heart-shaped stone in her hand and smiling. If she sent out that thought, maybe she would find the stone quicker. It couldn't hurt. For an instant an image of the stone flashed through her mind, but she couldn't hold it there long enough to understand it.

She left quickly and looked into the room across the hall. This one looked like a work room of some kind. There were tables with piles of weapons in various states of repair, giant odd-looking tools, piles of leather garments, tack for horses, chain mail, and gloves. And there was a chair at one of those tables that looked like the workman might be coming back. Frankie spun around, listened at the door, peeked out, and scampered farther down the empty hall toward the next door.

The next door was secured with a padlock, so she ignored it for the moment and went into the room across the hall.

Here was a room she recognized immediately: the laundry room. There were stacks of sheets and towels, and other laundry. Wash tubs stood at the end of the room and wash lines were strung from wall to wall. A spinning wheel and a big loom in the corner looked like someone had actually been using them.

Frankie was starting to feel like a ghost, walking through these rooms, seeing evidence that people lived and worked here, but not seeing anyone. Maybe they all went to the tournament? Frankie caught herself almost wishing to see someone. Don't send that thought out, thank you very much! To counteract it, she mentally envisioned that column of light again, surrounding her and keeping her safe from the eyes of others. As the vision got stronger, she began to feel warm and safe. She looked out into the hall again, saw that it was still empty, and trotted down to the next door.

This one was obviously a junk room, with broken furniture and china, old washboards, a few chairs, and a table with a leg missing. The room was filled with dust and dirt and cobwebs, and it was obvious that it wasn't often visited.

Frankie was stumped. She had reached the end of the hall and she hadn't found the storeroom she needed. Aradia had assured Ilayna, who had told Frankie. . . she checked her map again. She must be on the right floor. And the storeroom she wanted must be the room that was locked! What would she do now? She had to get in there. The sooner she got in, the sooner she could get out of here for good! Her skin started to crawl and she suddenly heard voices coming her way.

She pulled the door closed as she backed into the junk room. She looked frantically around to find something to hide behind. There! A huge chair with a high carved back was in the corner nearest the door. She climbed over a couple of pieces of furniture as quietly as she could and hid behind the chair.

The voices had settled into the rhythm of two people talking. It sounded like two girls. Probably two girls who worked in the fortress, Frankie thought. If they didn't work here, they would probably be out watching the tournament. They were walking past the door to the junk room now, and Frankie could hear what they were saying.

". . . someone accused her of spying for Lady Aradia, carryin' messages to those people in that other city. Poor Aldrid! They didn't even let her defend herself at all, they jest threw her in one o' them cells down there and left her!"

"But what are they gonna do to her? Will they ever let her out?"

"Not anytime soon, I'm thinking. There's something afoot around here, and I expect they'll keep the lockups closed right and tight until it's over, whatever it is they're up to. They won't want no trouble makers ruining their plans."

The voices faded as the girls turned the corner at the end of the hallway. Frankie was glad to hear them go. Even though she couldn't hear them anymore, she didn't move for about five minutes, just to be sure. The sudden arrival of real people had scared Frankie. She had really started to believe that she was alone in the fortress until she heard those voices. She wondered who poor Aldrid was and she felt sorry for her.

But she couldn't do much about it, and if she wasn't careful, she might get caught and have to join Aldrid in the dungeons. She climbed out from behind the big high-backed chair and listened at the door again. All was quiet. She looked out. No one to be seen. She tiptoed down the hall and stopped in front of the door with the padlock.

She looked closely at the lock. It was very, very old. Well, no. It was fairly new. But the style of the padlock, in Frankie's terms, was very, very old. It was big and square and had a large hole for a key right in the middle of its face. A metal piece looped up out of the lock on one side, threaded through two metal rings, one protruding out from each door, and locked back in to the other side of the padlock, keeping the doors tightly closed. How on earth could she get it unlocked? She pulled on it, just in case. No luck. It was firmly locked and it wasn't going to give.

Make it move! The words floated up from someplace near the pit of her stomach. Well, yes. If she could make a rock fly across Unarius' workroom, maybe she could make the padlock unlock itself. This was why she had practiced and practiced, over and over again, wasn't it? Frankie adjusted her headband so the crystal was right in the middle of her forehead. She looked quickly up and down the hall to be sure nothing was stirring. And then she focused her attention on the padlock. She envisioned how the lock must look behind the front plate, and she formed the words in her mind, "Unlock! Let go!"

Nothing happened. What was she going to do now? Maybe she could find something in the weapons room to pry it open? But it looked pretty sturdy, and besides, it would take some time and make some noise. Part of her very much wanted to just give it up and go home. Hey, she'd tried, hadn't she? But she knew, deep inside, that she couldn't just give up. *Try again!* This time, she felt it in her heart. Maybe she hadn't concentrated enough the first time? Or maybe she had concentrated too hard? She was scared, after all, and that was making it harder to focus her energy. Even as she looked around, Frankie could see the old grayish brown cloud welling up around her head.

"I love this lock and it's opening NOW!" she said in her mind, unfocusing her eyes and squinting sideways as she imagined all the atoms of the lock dancing away from each other. The lock started to vibrate. She kept imagining those dancing atoms and tried to imagine that she was dancing with them. The lock started to rattle. She could almost see the energy flowing from the middle of her forehead right into the center of the padlock. It shimmered, it shook, it rattled and then, *clunk!* It pulled itself open and hung there, as if it had been unlocked all along.

Frankie heard a sigh, and she wasn't sure if it came from her or the lock. She stared at it, afraid to believe what she saw. She reached over and picked the lock up in her hand. It really was unlocked! She pulled it out of the two metal rings on the doors, swung the doors open, and walked into the room.

She knew she'd found the right room, and she pulled the doors closed behind her. She looked around in awe. It was a combination of Uriel's lab and Unarius' workroom, but with a dull haze of thick dust and cobwebs over most of it. There were old books piled chest high, some as old and big as the big histories of Alaris that Unarius loved so much. There were musical instruments—a huge beautiful harp and a few stringed instruments she'd never seen before—sheet music, paintings. . . all the things that make life civilized and beautiful were hoarded and hidden away in this room.

A table shoved against one wall held a number of mortars and pestles, just like the ones Uriel used to crush her herbs, and there was jar upon jar of herbs and seeds and spices and leaves. Uriel and Ilayna would love to get their hands on this stuff, Frankie thought, whistling quietly under her breath. Another table held bottles of potions, various kinds of crockery and stirring and mixing implements, and hundreds of rocks, stones, and crystals of all different shapes, sizes, and colors. Toward the back of the room was a table with about 20 one- and two-foot-high crystal clusters with several long crystal points growing out of each base. These must be the crystals that could hold a person's energies.

Frankie cleared off the front of the table and pulled some of the big crystal clusters toward her. How was she to know which ones she wanted? She was looking for one that would somehow remind her of Aunt Cassie and one that she could somehow identify as Cybele. She had asked Unarius and Uriel how she would know which crystals to take, and both of them had told her the same, totally unhelpful, thing: "You'll know." Easy for them to say! The different parts of her mind all started shouting at once, and she was feeling very, very confused. What if she did it wrong?

You'll never be able to pick one, so just get out now while you can, one part of her screamed. Another part said, *Take them all and run!* But Frankie knew she could never carry them all. She took three deep breaths, quieted her mind as much as she could, and asked quietly under her breath what she should do. The answer floated up to her: *Pick one up and see.*

That sounded like a reasonable plan. She looked at the collection of crystals, all different sizes, shapes, and colors. A pale blue cluster that shimmered under the dust caught her attention. She didn't know what to do with it, so she picked it up and held it against her ear. She didn't hear anything, so she held it in front of her, against her heart, trying to focus her senses on the inside of the crystal. Frankie started to feel an energy around it, and a picture formed in her mind of a kind old woman. She reminded her of Uriel, even though she didn't look the same. She somehow felt like Uriel.

"Are you Cybele?" she asked, and then suddenly felt rather silly for asking. But when the answer *yes* seemed to whisper back, she didn't feel so silly after all, and her mind was suddenly filled with the laughing image of the younger woman in the portrait, the woman on the medallion.

All she had to do was break the cluster and Cybele would be free. That's what Aldebaran had said. But he warned her not to expect to see someone suddenly appear in front of her. He said that Frankie might see the wisp of energy escape from the pieces of crystal, but it would take some time before the energy would be able to reform into its bodily shape, if it did that at all. The energy might just float off to find its owner.

Frankie closed her eyes, held her breath, and dropped the beautiful crystal onto a small rug on the floor. Fortunately, the rug absorbed some of the impact, as Frankie had hoped, and the crystal didn't crash loudly.

Instead, it quietly dissolved into thousands of tiny shiny pieces that turned into a billow of energy, like a wisp of blue-green cloud, that spiraled up into the air. It floated past Frankie's cheek and, if she hadn't been able to see with her own eyes that there wasn't another person in the room, she would have sworn that someone kissed her as it floated past.

She looked around to find one that somehow made her think of Cassie. There! That one over there, the smallest one, that looked like the last remaining parts of a broken peach-colored crystal cluster. It only had two points, and there was a flat jagged place where the other four points should have been. *That's it!* She pulled it toward her and suddenly, in her head, she heard her Aunt Cassie's distinctive laugh. Of course this was it. This one, though, she had to keep. She wrapped it carefully in a piece of cloth and slipped it into her backpack. Aldebaran had told her not to break Aunt Cassie's crystal until she got it safely back home. Otherwise, that small part of her Aunt's energy might not be strong enough to make its way back through the portal alone.

Frankie looked around at the other smaller crystals and stones. There were hundreds of stones, but she did not see anything like the heart shaped pink one or the large double-terminated crystal that she had to find in order to lock the door between the worlds. Unarius had shown her a number of pictures of the quartz crystal, and he had shown her some smaller ones that he had at home, similar to the one she must find.

"Double terminated" meant it had a point at each end. This was even more important than the pink heart-shaped stone because the quartz crystal could lock the door against any other keys. It could also open the door against any other locks. It was like the master key and the deadbolt lock to the door between the worlds. But where was it? And where was the pink one? Frankie suddenly felt the wash of cold fear ooze down over her shoulders. If it was not here, Aradia had said, it would probably be in Janra's rooms. If Janra knew how important the key stones are, she might be keeping them with her personal things. Frankie didn't want to think about trying to go upstairs to get them, but she knew she had to do it.

She turned around and started to leave. Then she stopped. What if those other large quartz clusters held the energies of people, too, like Aunt Cassie and Cybele? As she thought about it, she had the impression of people crowding around her, begging her to let them out. She could almost hear the voices. Maybe she should smash those, too, and set them free?

She felt that it was something she wanted to do and she went back to the table.

She picked them up one at a time and held them momentarily against her heart, getting a feeling about the person, or energy, inside. Here was one that made her laugh, while this other one was sweet and loving. This amber one felt warm and friendly, this greenish one gave a feeling of healing.

Frankie picked them up one after the other and threw them to the floor. As they shattered, little wispy billows rose up around her, and she almost thought she heard soft little voices thanking her.

Frankie didn't stop to think too much about what she was doing, because she was afraid someone might come along and find her. She did stop, though, when she picked up a huge cluster of dark smoky quartz. All the others had been clear, with tinges of color. This one was a deep, dull, grayish black, and when she picked it up it was much heavier than the others. As she held it, she felt as if someone had reached into her chest and was squeezing the air out of her lungs. She had a sudden sharp pain in her chest and she could feel her heart thumping slowly and heavily. The hair on the back of her neck stood on end, her breath came in ragged gasps, and she broke out in goose pumps. Frankie suddenly noticed that the garnet in the silver bracelet Ilayna gave her had turned to a dark, muddy red. Ilayna had said it would change colors if it came into the presence of evil. And this crystal felt like evil! How many other signs did she need? Frankie started to put it back on the table, feeling a strong need to get away from it as fast as she could.

The huge chunk of smoky quartz suddenly seemed to squirm in her grasp, as if trying to escape, and Frankie started to drop it. She caught it tight against herself, and then wrestled it back onto the table. It didn't want to go back, and it fought her every inch of the way. It felt like it weighed a thousand pounds and Frankie was afraid she would drop it. She somehow knew that this was one crystal she didn't want to break open, because whoever or whatever was trapped inside had to be kept right where it was.

Once the black crystal was back on the table, Frankie stared at the thing, feeling slightly sick to her stomach. It beckoned her to pick it back up, and its commanding energy was hard to resist. It was as if it got into her head, making promises of rich rewards if Frankie would smash it on the floor and release its prisoner. For just the flicker of a moment, Frankie almost felt like it would be a good thing to smash that crystal, and that she could have everything she'd ever wanted if she just did that one thing. The thought of a life back home with her mother still alive floated softly into her mind for just an instant, and Frankie could feel a deep yearning in her heart as she started to reach for the crystal.

STOP! This time, the voices in her head yelled the same thing all at once. *STOP!* Frankie jerked away, as if waking up suddenly from a dream, feeling a bit uncertain and groggy. She managed to shake it off and backed up slowly across the room, keeping an eye on the hulking dark crystal every inch of the way, until she finally felt the door against her back.

She stopped and listened: no sounds coming from the hall. She went out into the hall and refastened the padlock, feeling much better to have that thing in the smoky quartz safely locked up. Who—or what—was in that crystal, she wondered as the lock clicked into place. A name suddenly floated into her mind: *Belzar!*

Frankie was astonished. Could the essence of that black-haired woman who battled Aunt Cassie be caught up in that hulking black crystal? Could she have somehow saved herself and found her way inside a crystal for protection, even though her body had been mortally wounded in the fight? Why not? Why not, indeed? Frankie shuddered at the thought and remembered how it felt, struggling with that heavy crystal, and feeling that dark, destructive energy all around it, reaching into her mind. In her own way, Frankie had just fought Belzar, too. And, fortunately, she, too, had won.

Frankie leaned against the door and took a deep breath. She checked to be sure that her backpack was zipped, with Aunt Cassie's crystal deep inside, and swung the straps over her shoulders. She leaned back, closed her eyes, and allowed a mental picture to fill her mind. She envisioned the pink heart-shaped stone and the double-terminated quartz crystal key. She envisioned her hand reaching out and picking them up. She let herself feel how excited and satisfied she would feel to have found them. She savored the moment. She couldn't quite see where they were, but she felt that she would find them now. She let go of the vision then turned and walked toward the stairway at the end of the hall. It was time to find Janra's rooms.

15

The Crystal Key

*A*t the top of the stairs, two flights up, Frankie stood in the doorway and looked down a long hallway. It was as long as the one she had been in downstairs, but it looked quite different. She had been here before. Her palms felt suddenly clammy as she remembered this hall from her horror-filled interview with Janra. STOP! She admonished herself. Don't focus on that or you just might repeat it!

It was still gruesome. Instead of the beautiful paintings that she had seen in the storeroom, the walls were decorated with sets of weapons and the stuffed and mounted heads of animals. Frankie shuddered, not wanting to even step foot in the hallway.

She could hear an occasional roar from the crowd at the tournament, like hearing a football game from a few blocks away, but she was relieved to hear no sounds of activity nearby. About halfway down the hall on the left were heavy dark wooden double doors with a gold and red rug in front of them. On each side of the doorway there were large pillars that looked sort of silly in the middle of the other barbaric decorations. But it was obvious that it must be the most important room on this hallway. It must be Janra's room.

Frankie reminded herself to pull in all her energy again, then she pulled the cloak tight around her and crept down the hall.

The first room had a crude table with several plain wooden chairs. The table held several plain metal candlesticks with half-burned candle stubs in them and the remains of a half-eaten bowl of fruit. The bread plate next to it held only crumbs and the drops of wine left in the metal goblet smelled dank and sour. The only decorations in the room were weapons hung here and there, and a hideous tapestry on one wall depicting a woman warrior on horseback spearing a unicorn. Frankie tried not to look.

Frankie went through a connecting door into a bedroom. There was a big Spartan bed with a lumpy mattress, a pillow and a dark gray wool blanket that looked like it would really itch. There were two plain wooden chairs and a big wardrobe. A small table in the corner boasted an old mirror in a dark wooden frame and a surprisingly pretty wash bowl and pitcher, painted dark blue with flowers. They were the only touch of brightness in the dark, uncomfortable room, so different from the elegant but simple comfort at Uriel's house.

Frankie went over to take a closer look at the bowl and pitcher. They were heavy stoneware rather than delicate china, but someone had taken the time to paint the flowers. She poured some of the water into the bowl, filled her cupped hands, and splashed it on her face. The water felt cool and sharpened her senses.

As she moved to leave, Frankie looked down without thinking, and she caught sight of an image in the water bowl. She was scrying an image of herself! She saw herself standing in a totally different room, one that she had never seen before. She watched herself lift up the edge of a huge tapestry on the wall and walk behind it. Instead of forming a lump under the tapestry, she completely disappeared and the tapestry settled back flat against the wall. Frankie wanted to watch some more, to figure out where the room was and what she was doing there, but she suddenly heard voices and the image faded.

She nearly knocked the bowl over as she jumped, but managed to catch it as she looked around frantically for someplace to hide. What was she going to do? There was no point in trying to hide under the bed. It was too high off the floor, and there were no linens hanging over the sides to shield her from view. The wardrobe! It was the only place! The voices came closer as she sprinted across the room.

"I wish we could go see the jousting," someone was complaining.

Frankie managed to pull the wardrobe door mostly closed before the two girls came in. She recognized the voices as the same ones she had heard downstairs.

"Well, if you hadna spilled ale on that man, you mighta been spared," the second girl said. "I'm lucky I din't get whipped for takin' that knife. I was jest gonna use it to cut that apple I saved. But they was in a good mood this mornin' so's they let me go. They jest made me work today, like you, as a punishment. I hope that's all they's gonna do!"

"Yeah. They mighta put us in the dungeons like poor Aldrid!"

The girls fussed around the room for a few minutes in silence, tidying up, making the bed, and dusting. Through the crack of the open wardrobe door, Frankie saw one of them dump the water from the bowl out the window, while the other shook out the heavy gray blanket, folded it, and placed it back on the bed.

They wore rather plain brownish shapeless dresses that were homespun cloth. Frankie wondered if the cloth was made on that big loom downstairs. Their garments did not show the color of their energy, like the clothing materials in Alaris. But Frankie was surprised that she could see bits of colored energy coming out around their heads. There was definitely a hazy, yellowish-brown glow that came out about two inches all around their heads.

Recalling her lessons about energy colors, Frankie decided the girls were probably relatively harmless. She didn't think they would try to hurt her if they found her, but they might cause trouble by screaming or calling for help if she startled them.

One of the girls started to walk toward the wardrobe. "I'm gonna look in here and see if there's anything. . ."

What could Frankie do? If that girl found her. . . Frankie's head was suddenly filled with visions of being trapped in the wardrobe with the two girls screaming down the hallways until all the warriors came in from the field and. . . CUT IT OUT! She caught herself in mid-thought. Don't think about that! Think about what you *want* to have happen!

Remembering her practice with poor Sebastian the cat, Frankie stared through the tiny crack at the girl and thought as strongly as she could, "GO AWAY! GET OUT OF HERE! GO AWAY! NOW! IT'S DANGEROUS HERE! RUN AWAY!" Frankie tried to envision both girls leaving the room, but she couldn't form a clear mental picture because she was too scared. But she kept holding the thought and she saw a faint wisp of orange vapor seep out of the wardrobe and reach out toward the girl as the words formed in her head.

The girl stopped in mid-step and shivered, almost as if she felt Frankie's thoughts. She shook her head and looked confused, then she turned around to her friend and said, "Do you get a bad feelin' 'bout this room?"

"Whatcha mean?"

"I dunno. But I don' like it in here. We're done, so maybe

we should go on now. Maybe there's a ghost or something in here. I dunno, I jest don't like it."

She turned on her heel and headed for the door, grabbing the other girl by the wrist and dragging her along with her. The other girl protested, but she went along.

Frankie counted to ten after they left, and then slowly opened the wardrobe door. She was drenched in sweat even though it was not particularly hot in there. She felt nearly faint from the idea that she had almost been discovered. Maybe she should just run while she had the chance? Several voices in her head loudly agreed with that idea. But she took a deep breath, calmed herself, and the answer came drifting up to her mind from deep inside. *You have to go on,* it said. And she knew it was true.

She went to the doorway of the outer room, paused, and listened. There wasn't a sound. She peeked out the door and looked down the hall. There was no one in sight, but as she stared, she saw a disturbance in the air in front of a door down the hall, almost like the sun glinting off a unicorn horn. Could it be? Frankie didn't think so. But the thought of Aldebaran gave her courage. She sprinted down the hall toward that door, knowing it would lead to Janra's room. The door was open. And she went in.

It wasn't what she expected, but then she wasn't exactly sure what she expected. Nothing in this strange world could have been expected. And everything in Kelghard seemed slightly off, slightly wrong, as if the people who first came here couldn't quite remember how it was supposed to be. Perhaps Frankie had expected to find herself in the room she had been brought to before. She was glad this wasn't it.

Janra's room was huge. It looked vaguely familiar, but Frankie didn't know why. There was a giant, beautifully woven tapestry that covered one entire wall, depicting a huge bloody battle. On the opposite wall was a large fireplace that a person could walk into, with a hip-high brass lion guarding each side. A large desk dominated this end of the room and an ornately carved four-poster bed with heavy drapes dominated the far end. The other furniture was heavy and dark and intricately carved. There were dozens of candles in tall gold and silver candle holders, but they weren't lit. Several narrow slit windows provided some light, but didn't completely dispel the gloom.

Everywhere she looked, Frankie saw objects that must have been stolen from Alaris. They were displayed like trophies on the long, carved mantle and on shelves that looked specially built for that purpose. The objects in the storeroom had apparently been stored for a long time ago, because they had been covered in thick dust. Here, the crystals and musical instruments and prisms and piles of books were clean, as if they were used and well kept. Some items were laid out on a long carved table, as though they were being inspected. Uriel had said that Janra's men had been raiding more often in the past few months—and Frankie wondered if this was where they brought the loot. Frankie also wondered if Janra had found what she was looking for: a clue to the location of the door between the worlds and a key to open the door.

Frankie walked deeper into the room, drawn as if by a magnet to a large chest that sat on the floor at the foot of the bed. The top of the trunk was pushed back, and the chest was so full that its contents tumbled out into a pile on the floor. It reminded her of an old pirate's chest, filled to overflowing with all kinds of treasure: jewels, goblets, knives, and precious stones. Frankie raked her hand through the pile, picking up and inspecting different pieces of jewelry and stones that caught her eye.

When her eye paused on one particular stone, the hair on the back of her neck stood on end. It was a clear quartz crystal, shaped like a short, fat wand, with six flat sides and a point at each end. The stone seemed to glow, as if there was a live star trapped inside. This was the master key to the door between the worlds! Frankie was absolutely sure! It seemed to call to her: *Here I am, take me with you.* She picked it up and felt a shock run from her fingertips to her toes. With tingling fingers, Frankie took a piece of loose fabric from the trunk and wrapped it around the crystal, then put it carefully in her backpack with Aunt Cassie's crystal.

Now all she had to do was find the pink heart-shaped stone and get out. It really wasn't as important as the clear crystal, she knew, but somehow she felt attached to it in some way, and she didn't want to leave it here with these barbarians. She wanted to take it home with her and put it back where it belonged, in its place on the picture frame. Frankie stopped and listened, but didn't hear anyone coming. It couldn't hurt to look for just another minute. She searched through the trunk but couldn't find it. Come to me, little pink stone, Frankie thought to herself. But it just wasn't there.

She was starting to doubt that she would find it and suddenly it didn't matter, because someone was coming down the hall. Someone who was very angry, from the sound of her voice. . . from the sound of that voice that Frankie remembered all too vividly. Frankie took a few steps, then froze in place.

"What do you mean, that strange girl is gone? I won't have it!" Janra's voice boomed and reverberated down the long hall, making Frankie wince from the energy of it.

She looked frantically around for a hiding place. This room had no handy wardrobe to hide in, and none of the pieces of furniture would protect her, either.

"She may not have gone far on her own, my Mistress," a man's voice responded. He sounded scared and pleading. "I am sure she will return soon."

Frankie was scared, too, because she didn't know what to

do. BE CALM! she told herself. There is a place in this room to hide, a place that is safe. Where is it? She waited. She tried to calm her mind. It wasn't working. Doubt and fear had grabbed hold of her and all she could think of was the orange sparks that could shoot from Janra's fingers, and the long thin knife she kept in her boot.

An idea forced its way into her mind and she felt what seemed like a gentle nudge at the small of her back: *The trunk. Hide behind the trunk.* Maybe the upraised lid would protect her from view? Some screaming part of her said it would never work. Her heart said it would. She had nothing to lose, because she had nowhere else to hide. She scurried behind it, between the trunk and the bed, under the upraised lid. She yanked her backpack off and pulled it in against her chest, and she tucked the edges of the cloak around her. At that moment, Janra thundered into the room, the man trailing behind her.

"Do not try to placate me, you fool. Who told you she's gone?" Janra demanded. She started pacing back and forth in the middle of the room.

Frankie tried to calm herself, and she mentally pulled all her energy inside her. If they can't sense your energy, they won't notice you. That was what Ilayna said, that was the idea behind making herself invisible. But she'd never had to try it when it really counted. She didn't think it was working. She tried again. She imagined her energy flowing around herself, glowing and pulsing. Then she pictured it flowing back into her body, being drawn in, being absorbed. It *had* to work. It *would* work!

"The spy's sister agreed to observe the girl for us," the man said. "She hopes to get her sister back unharmed. She has no reason to lie, because if she does. . ." He laughed a nasty, high-pitched, mean kind of laugh that told Frankie that both girls would be severely punished either way. These guys wouldn't keep their end of the bargain.

Frankie peeped out around the corner of the trunk and was surprised to see a dense, dark, blue-gray cloud around Janra's head, with what looked like red arrows of anger shooting out of it in all directions. It looked like a storm cloud. The man had a cloud around his head, too, but it was grayer and browner than Janra's. Frankie was sure that he was terrified of Janra and what she might do to him. And she suddenly realized what they meant when they said those emotion clouds were infectious. Frankie could actually feel his fear, as if it were creeping up her arms, magnifying her own fear. It wasn't a good sign.

"What did she say? What did she see?" Janra demanded.

"She said the girl from the other world left the house first, alone. The others left later, the herb woman, the old man, and Lady Aradia's daughter. We think their destinations were not the same, or they would have left together."

Janra stopped pacing. "A pox on Aradia and her daughter. Those scheming traitors!" she thundered. "It took me months to find this stupid rock in those old books," she took something out of her pocket and waved it toward a stack of old books next to the desk. "Now that I know that this is the Key, I must find that child! She is the only one who can show me the Door to Other Worlds. We've been preparing for this for years. I, Janra, the Mistress of All I Survey, will conquer those other lands, and I, Janra, will be the Mistress of All the Worlds!"

She looked like she was going to shove the thing down the poor man's throat to make her point, and Frankie was stunned to see that the thing she was waving around was the pink heart-shaped stone!

"But this child," Janra shrieked, "this child MUST BE FOUND! I MUST HAVE HER! NOW! NO EXCUSES!"

"Yes, my Mistress." The man started to back out of the room, bowing low in Janra's direction as he went. "I will send riders out to find her immediately."

"You just do that, Caius, because I want her brought here tonight. On your life, Caius! Do you hear me? Tomorrow we go through that Door to Other Worlds and we attack!"

The man practically fell over as he scrambled to get out, and Janra started after him.

Oh no, thought Frankie, peeking out after her, shouting in her head, "JANRA, LEAVE THE PINK STONE HERE. LEAVE IT HERE! DROP IT! DROP IT NOW!"

Janra hesitated in the doorway, stopped and looked down at the stone in her hand, then she turned around and tossed it into the overflowing trunk. Then she headed back toward the doorway. As Frankie started to breathe easier, she heard the worst words she'd ever heard: "You! Stay here and guard this door! No one, do you hear me, *no one* is to go in, or I'll have your head for breakfast!"

She was trapped.

16

Escape to the Dungeon

When Frankie could breathe again, the first thing she did was crawl out from behind the trunk and grab the pink heart-shaped stone from the top of the pile where Janra had tossed it. Then she put it into one of the zippered pockets of her backpack and pulled the zipper closed. She patted the small hard bulge and smiled. Then she looked toward the door. Janra had not bothered to close the door and the guard was apparently just outside in the hall. What was she going to do?

BE CALM! That was the first thing to do. She was so scared, she could barely think. But there had to be another way out of here. She had Aunt Cassie's crystal, she had the master key crystal, and she had the pink heart-shaped stone. She had found everything she had come here to find, and she had not gone through all this just to get trapped in Janra's bedroom!

There's a way out of here, Frankie told herself. Where is it?

The first thing she did was pull in all her energy again, willing herself to become invisible to the guard at the door. Then she carefully inspected the room, looking for the way out. The tall narrow windows had bars. No escape that way. And there was no other door. She looked around at the cluttered room and felt despair well up in her chest. She tried not to think about being captured and tortured by the Mistress of All the Worlds, but it was hard. She giggled at the titles Janra gave herself, and that made her feel a little better.

The large tapestry on one wall caught her eye, and she wondered why it looked vaguely familiar. Frankie tiptoed over to it and looked at it more carefully. Where had she seen it before? She felt it was important but she couldn't figure out why. She felt so overwhelmed she just couldn't think. She forced herself to take in three deep breaths, letting each one out very slowly, and tried to let her mind be very calm and quiet. She had to do it two more times before she actually felt she could breathe.

What did she know about this tapestry? Slowly, like the details of a half-remembered dream, it came back to her. It was the tapestry she had seen when she suddenly looked and saw her own image in the water bowl in the bedroom down the hall, before the maids came in. Why had she seen that image? What was so important about the tapestry?

Calm down, Frankie, she told herself, it'll come, it's almost here. Just relax and let it come. Several voices in her head started shrieking and she told them to shut up.

She looked at the tapestry again. It was huge. The ceiling was very high and the tapestry extended from about a foot below the ceiling down to about a foot above the floor. She made herself carefully look at every section of the tapestry, moving her vision from the top to the bottom and back up again. Nothing about the tapestry caught her eye. Then, as she was looking down a section of tapestry almost halfway down its length, something tugged at her attention. Down by the bottom edge she noticed a funny crack running up the wall from the floor. There was another one about three feet farther down the wall. She pondered. Two parallel cracks in the wall going up from the floor and disappearing behind the tapestry. What does that mean? Wait! Wait! It's coming! She suddenly had the image in her mind that she had seen before. She saw herself go behind the tapestry and disappear! That must mean. . . a door! Those two cracks marked a hidden door behind the tapestry! Exhilaration leaped up, only to fall back again as she pondered the next big question: where does it lead? It doesn't matter.

Frankie had to get down on her knees to pull the edge of the tapestry away from the wall and look behind it. She could see the whole outline of the door, and there, half-way up, was a sliding bolt lock. She crawled up under and behind the heavy tapestry and stood up. It banged back against her, forcing her face-first into the door. She was closed in completely by the heavy, thick tapestry, and Frankie suddenly felt like she was suffocating. It was like being caught at the bottom of the bed under the covers—only worse—and she started to feel all turned around and dizzy, as if she didn't know which way was out. If she didn't get out of here soon, she thought, she would start to scream.

She forced herself to take two steps backward, slowly. She could feel the tapestry resist, as if it wanted to keep her trapped, but finally it gave way and seemed to crawl heavily up her back and across the back of her head as she forced it with her body out and away from the wall. That was better. A little bit of light and air swirled up and in, and she took a breath.

She reached over and slid the bolt to the right, releasing it. Then she looked for a knob or handle to pull the door open. But there was nothing. What now? A door was no good if it wouldn't open. And she couldn't stand there very long, with the suffocating weight of the tapestry pressing down on her, trying to find a hidden handle. But what else could she do?

She thought about trying to squeeze herself through the bars on the windows, but she knew that wouldn't work. Even if she could do it, she'd end up falling three flights to the ground. The only other thing she could think of was to make a mad dash out the door, trying to use surprise and speed to get her past the guard before he could react enough to catch her. It was a slim chance, but it was the only one she might have. Frankie raised her fist and beat against the door in total frustration.

Something gave and it swung open.

She almost pitched forward because the weight of the tapestry at her back propelled her along, but she stopped herself from plunging into the dark void. It took her a minute to focus her eyes. What she saw, vaguely outlined in the dim light seeping in under the tapestry, was a narrow landing and a flight of stone steps going down. It didn't look very inviting. And it was really dark. Frankie didn't know where they went, but she realized it didn't matter. It was the only way out.

She went all the way in and approached the top step. The tapestry thumped against the wall and the door swished closed behind her. Now it was pitch black. It was also very cold and very damp. And Frankie was very, very scared. She had so many voices screaming inside her head that she thought she would start screaming, too. She shook her head and mentally commanded them to stop.

She stood on the landing for a few minutes trying to adjust her eyes to the pitch black all around her. She couldn't even see the steps, and she was glad that she had seen them at least once before even that dim light was cut off. She swung her backpack over both her shoulders and rebalanced her weight. She concentrated on the thought that she was safe and all was well, and she just held that thought for a couple of minutes and breathed. Then she slowly started to feel her way along. She really wished she had thought to bring one of those wonderful flashlight crystals with her, but she hadn't, and there was nothing she could do about it now. She was also disappointed that her headband didn't help.

She reached out to the two sides of the stairwell and placed one hand flat against each wall. The stone was surprisingly cold and damp under her fingers. And there was a moldy smell that made her nose stuffy. With her right toe she tapped at the stone under her foot, inching her toe forward slowly until it hit air instead of stone. A step. She lowered her foot onto the step below and moved her left foot down to join it. Then she repeated the process. Tapping the stone underfoot, inching forward, feeling air, stepping down with her left foot. Starting again with the right foot.

Over and over and over she did it, until she thought she would start screaming or go crazy or both. If there was one thing she hated more than being trapped in the dark, it was being trapped in a small enclosed place. This was both. In the total darkness, she had no concept of time. She didn't know if she was in there for five minutes or five days. The steps just went on and on. She started to think she would be locked up in this black moldy damp darkness until she died.

But she didn't let that stop her. She just kept on tapping with her foot, inching ahead, feeling air, and stepping down for what seemed like weeks. Until she finally tapped and tapped and inched and inched and still felt stone under her feet, and her toe couldn't go any farther forward. She had lost count a long time ago, after the fifty-second step, but she was finally at the bottom. Now what?

Frankie moved her hands over the walls, palms flat and fingers splayed, feeling around to her right, to her left, in front of her. She moved around so much that she lost track of her direction and she almost fell face forward into the steps she'd just come down. And then she finally found a door with a small sliding lock, like the one upstairs.

She wanted to jerk it open and run screaming out the door, gasping for air. But she didn't. Once she had her fingers curled around the metal lock, she forced herself to stop and breathe slowly, to calm herself and relax. She had no idea what was behind that door. She might be walking right into the warriors' locker room or something, for all she knew. She did not allow herself to believe that *anyplace* would be better than here, because she was well aware that some places would be worse. She pulled in her energy, envisioned herself wrapped in a column of light, and she reminded herself to be cautious and go slowly.

Frankie put her ear against the door, but she couldn't hear anything. She slid the lock open and pulled. Nothing happened. The door didn't give an inch and she knew that if it didn't open in a very short time she really would start screaming. She took in another deep breath. She put her hands flat against the door and tried pushing softly. The door swung out about an inch.

She had expected a flood of light, but it appeared that the room beyond the door was dimly lit. She still didn't hear anything, so she pushed the door open farther and looked out.

She heard a gasp, looked up, and saw a girl standing against the opposite wall with her arms up in the air. Their eyes held for a minute—it seemed like ten—and neither of them moved. Frankie realized that the girl couldn't move because she was chained to the wall. Frankie realized she had found the dungeon, the one place in the whole fortress she had promised herself she would avoid. And here was this poor girl. She must be Aldrid, the one the maids had talked about. The one who spied for Aradia. The one whose sister went to spy on Frankie to get her free. Frankie could see why.

The place was a square room with a tiny barred window up near the ceiling. Frankie knew she'd gone down a lot of steps in that dark stairway to end up down here. There were chains and heavy handcuffs attached to the walls. Aldrid's hands were caught in two of them, above her head. It looked horribly uncomfortable. The floor was covered with filthy straw that reeked of spoiled food, and worse. It smelled worse than a summer camp latrine on a hot August day. Frankie thought she was going to throw up as an acid taste started to work its way up her throat. But there was a quick movement that diverted her attention to the right: a rat. A huge gray rat. Frankie recoiled as it ran toward a man who was also in handcuffs. He was slumped down and his eyes were closed. At least he wasn't a guard.

Frankie felt like she couldn't possibly be seeing what she was seeing. She couldn't possibly be here, in a real dungeon. It couldn't possibly be worse than she had imagined, but it was. She couldn't possibly be standing in front of someone her own age chained to a wall, but she was. Who *are* these people?

She was so overwhelmed that she felt like collapsing on the floor in tears. But she knew that wouldn't help anything, so she pulled herself together. This was her road to travel and she had to believe that she could do it. She had to! The voices in her head were strangely quiet. Maybe they were overwhelmed, too.

"Are you Aldrid?" Frankie whispered, and was almost surprised that her voice still worked.

The girl just looked at her and nodded.

"I won't hurt you. I'm Frankie. I'm a friend of Aradia and Ilayna."

She hoped Aldrid wouldn't be mad about that, especially since she had been thrown in here for helping Aradia. But Aldrid's face immediately brightened.

"I knew Lady Aradia wouldn't leave me to rot in here, I jest knew it," she said. "She's a real lady, she is, even if she is Janra's sister."

"These dungeons are horrible," Frankie said, moving

across the room to inspect the girl's manacles and chains. "Are you all right?"

"I might be better, I might be worse," Aldrid answered, "but I can say I've been in better places. This is Mistress Janra's private dungeon, for her special cases. You get special attention when you get put in here." The girl gave a bitter laugh and then choked.

Frankie could barely listen. She didn't want to hear about this girl getting special attention from Janra, or think about the special attention she would get if she got caught. She rallied herself again. "Well, wherever we are, we have to figure out how to get you out of those handcuffs and get us both out of here."

"Ain't no way, miss, if you don't have a key, unless you find the warder. He'll be back with my dinner soon and if he catches you, he'll lock you up too.

"But don't feel bad," the girl continued, "nobody could get these cuffs off without a key. I won't blame you for going ahead. The Lady will get me out, you'll see. I'm not worried."

Frankie admired her ability to be optimistic while she was chained to a wall in a dungeon. "I'm not going to leave you here, if I can help it. But just be quiet so I can think a minute. There has to be a way to get those chains off your wrists, and off his, too."

"Oh," the girl said, dropping her voice, "you don't have to worry any about him, miss. He's beyond helping."

Frankie looked at the man. He hadn't moved. He would never move again. If Frankie had not understood the kind of people she was dealing with before, she did now. And, despite her brave words, Frankie figured that Aldrid would be like that before long if Frankie didn't help her. But voices were screaming in her head, telling her to run away and not look back.

After she forced herself to be calm again, the first thing

that occurred to her was to try to get the cuffs to unlock, the way she did with the padlock downstairs—or upstairs, or wherever that was. She tried to concentrate, to direct her focus and her energy and her will to one of them, but she knew it just wasn't going to work. And it didn't. She was too worried and distracted to do it properly. She tried pulling on it, but she knew before she started that wouldn't work, either. Aldrid had been pulling on them for days. Maybe she could find something to use as a lever to pry it open? She looked around. No luck.

Frankie sighed and leaned against the wall, her arms crossed in front of her. There had to be a way. If only she could focus better, or magnify the energy. What could she do? The headband wasn't working. And if she didn't do something soon, the jailer would be back, and she would either be caught in Janra's private cell or trapped in that stairway again. Either way, she was caught.

She stuck her hand in her backpack and patted the crystals. At least she had those. But she had to get them out of here. Maybe she should concentrate on finding a way out, and just leave Aldrid to her fate? Which was more important? She didn't want to have to choose.

Suddenly she remembered that clear crystals magnify energy, and she had the king of them all right there in her backpack. If that crystal wand couldn't magnify her energy, nothing could. Even at home they used crystals in radio transmitters and laser beams, didn't they? Between the crystal wand and the headband, it might work. It was worth a try.

Frankie carefully unwrapped the large double-terminated crystal and held one end to the headband on her forehead and pointed the other end right at one of the large metal cuffs. Aldrid looked at her like she was crazy, but Frankie just ignored her and started to concentrate. She threw her concentration through the crystal, issuing her thought commands toward the locked handcuff: OPEN! COME LOOSE! OPEN!

It didn't work. She tried again, thinking of all the little atoms dancing to the far sides of the room. OPEN! OPEN! OPEN! Time seemed to stand still and Frankie was concentrating so hard on that handcuff that she felt like she had become part of it. Time stopped and the room swirled.

The sudden *clunk!* of the metal handcuff dropping open startled her so much that she almost dropped the crystal. Aldrid burst into tears.

"Are you a witch?" she screamed. It sounded like she'd rather be back in the handcuff and chains than saved by a witch!

"No I'm not a witch!" Frankie snarled at her. "Now be quiet while I do the other one!"

The second one didn't take as long as the first, but just as they heard the opening clunk, they also heard the scrape of a key in the outside door.

"Put your arms back up, and be quiet," Frankie growled at Aldrid through her teeth. Still clutching the pointed crystal, she grabbed up her backpack and jumped back through the door to the stairs, leaving it open a tiny crack. She could see Aldrid from there, and she knew she had to think of some way to get rid of the jailer and get the two of them through that door, outside, and free.

Aldrid was still shaken from watching Frankie open the handcuffs, but she had the presence of mind to grab them up around her wrists and put her arms up the way they had been, to make it appear that they were still locked.

"Here's some bread for ye," the man said, after kicking the door closed with his foot. "I ain't going to feed ye agin, seeing as ya spit it out in me face the las' time. After that yer lucky I brought ye anything! But me wife says as yer a good lass, though, an' ye prolly din't do much of anything to earn this penance, so I'll let ye have one hand down to eat. But if ye try anything this time. . ."

He kept talking and Frankie realized that his unexpected kindness toward Aldrid could ruin everything. If he tried to unlock one of the handcuffs to let Aldrid eat, he would discover that both of them were already unlocked. She didn't want to think about how hard it must be for poor Aldrid, holding her arms up above her head, pretending she was still caught. Frankie knew she had to think of something fast.

She didn't have time to think of anything, because the idea flowed into her mind in the same moment that the jailer walked over and put his back to her. And in that same moment she pushed the door open against him as hard as she could possibly shove it. It caught him in the back with a thud. He grunted, then he fell forward onto the stone floor, hitting his head. She would have hit him with the crystal if she'd had to, but she didn't: He didn't move.

Faster than she thought she could ever move, Frankie shoved the crystal and her headband into her backpack, zipped it shut, slung the pack over her shoulder, grabbed Aldrid, and dragged her toward the door.

"Are there more guards?" she asked in a whisper.

"No, he's it. Them others went out to see the festival," Aldrid whispered back.

Frankie threw the door open. The hallway in front of her was dank and murky, but she was relieved to see sunlight pouring in through grated openings in the opposite wall. It felt like she had been locked up in the cold and dark for days. And now she was almost free. All they had to do was follow the hallway through the dungeon, find the stairs, and get back to the stables. Frankie was so excited about getting out of Janra's room and setting Aldrid free, that getting out of the fortress almost seemed easy. But she had to get going, now!

Aldrid stood in the doorway, completely paralyzed.

Frankie grabbed her arm and pulled. "Let's go. We have to get out of here. NOW, ALDRID, MOVE."

But Aldrid was transfixed by the rumble of voices that came rolling past them like a big wave from the fields. The tournament! Frankie had completely forgotten. She started to hear other noises, more movement in the fortress than she had heard before. Was the tournament over? Were people starting to come back from the fields? With everyone's focus on the tournament, Frankie had felt safe. But now she may have lost her advantage.

She spun around and faced Aldrid. "Aldrid, where are the stables from here?"

"Stables," Aldrid repeated, as if she'd never heard of such a thing. Then it registered. "Oh, they're in the courtyard."

"I know that. How do I get there?"

"You mean. . .?"

"Which direction? Do I go down the hall this way or the other way?"

"Oh, ye'd best go this way," Aldrid pointed right. "When ye come to the staircase, go up three flights and it's there."

Frankie mentally pictured where she needed to go, then pictured herself jumping up into the cart and driving away, out the main gate. The sound of people brought her attention back to the moment.

"You have a choice, Aldrid, and you have to make it now. Come with me out of the fortress or stay here and fend for yourself. I have to go. Now."

Aldrid looked at her, taking her in from head to foot. The cloak was hanging open and Aldrid could see what she was wearing underneath. She looked at Frankie's sneakers, her jeans, her sweater, and her backpack. She'd never seen anything like them. She remembered that crystal headband. She looked back at the open wrist cuffs on the wall and back at Frankie. The word *witch* floated into Frankie's mind.

"You can't stay here," Frankie said as she saw Aldrid make that decision.

"Yes I can." Aldrid said flatly, pulling her arm away and stepping back into the cell. "I dunno who you are or where you're goin'. But I don't think I want to go there with you. I don't think it's my place. Besides, I don't have the strength. I'd only slow you down."

Frankie was tempted, but she just couldn't leave the girl here. "Come on," she said, "I'll help you. We can make it. Ilayna left a horse and cart for me. We can both leave in that."

"Lady Ilayna?" Aldrid seemed to waiver again. "She's a fine one, too, isn't she?" She paused again. "No," she continued, "I got an idea. You go on, and close the door behind ya. I'll wait and give you some time. Then I'll get myself away from here, too. Even if someone comes, they'll think I'm still in here chained to the wall. And if I have to, I'll put my arms back up over my head and show 'em. But I don't think anyone's gonna pay any mind to who's in here. Folks don't want to look too much at Mistress Janra's private doings. I'll bide here a bit and when it's time, I'll get away. Don't you worry. I have places to hide, safe as can be."

Frankie didn't really believe her, but she couldn't force her, and she knew she had to go. She looked at the jailer, who was still lying on the floor, out cold. Frankie was afraid she might have killed him.

Aldrid laughed. "He's not dead, that one. But he'll sure sleep for a time. Don't you worry, miss, I won't let that one stop me. I'll be long gone afore he wakes up." She looked at Frankie and smiled. "Go on. I'm not going with you."

Frankie gave Aldrid a quick hug, then turned on her heel and disappeared into the shadows.

❤   ❤   ❤

Frankie quickly navigated the hallway, keeping her head down to avoid seeing into any other cells. She climbed the stairway without seeing anyone, and she had started to relax again when she reached the courtyard and saw a knot of people milling about. Even if she could get to Daisy and the cart without anyone noticing her, how would she steer through these people and get safely out the gate? Where was Ilayna when she needed her? But Ilayna was nowhere to be seen.

Frankie ducked back into the shadows of the stairway. She adjusted the cape around her, closing it to cover her clothes, and pulling the hood up around her face. She pulled in her energy and forced herself to walk toward the stables as if she belonged there.

Just as Jaimie promised, the horse and cart were ready to go. Daisy whinnied a greeting when she got close, but no one seemed to notice. Frankie threw her backpack up under the seat and climbed in, grabbing the reins. Daisy started to move and then stopped. She looked around at Frankie as if waiting for instructions.

Frankie didn't know what to do. She hadn't mentioned to Ilayna that she'd never driven a horse and cart before. She had assumed Ilayna would be with her. Now she was on her own, and she didn't know what to do.

"Oh, there ye are," Jamie said as he walked up with a bag of feed. "Lady Ilayna ain't back yet. You takin' Daisy by yerself, then?"

Frankie nodded.

"Ye'd better pull up on them reins or Daisy'll jest drop her head and try to eat."

Frankie didn't know whether to laugh or cry, and there were parts of her that wanted to do both. She had to get out of here without being caught. She had to drive this cart, but she didn't know how.

Oh, give me some help here! She shouted the plea inside her head as she tried to think about what to do. And then an idea popped into her mind.

"Jamie," she said, "could you help me steer Daisy down to the gatehouse? I'm afraid with all these people." She could see more and more people entering the courtyard. They were in festive moods, shouting to each other and laughing, talking about the great feats they had seen at the tournament.

Jamie looked at her for a minute, thought about it, and then shrugged. "I can help ye, miss," he said as he swung up beside her on the bench seat. "I takes good care of Daisy for Lady Ilayna, and I guess I'll take good care of you, too." He gave her a big crooked grin, and Frankie could see that he had a tooth missing. She could also see that he probably knew that she didn't belong here and that he was taking a chance helping her get away.

Frankie grinned back, handed over the reins, and gave his hand a quick squeeze.

Then they were off. Frankie shoved her sneakered feet under the seat as far as they would go and pulled the cloak around her while Jamie slowly led Daisy through the crowd. People sensed them coming and moved away without paying any attention. Frankie figured that Jamie was the best cover she could have found, and she sent out a silent Thank You!

As they reached the outer bailey, they fell in with another crowd of people who were also making their way to the gatehouse to leave Kelghard. It was slow progress, but Frankie felt calm, counting on Jamie to get them through. She wondered what she would do when Jamie had to leave her, but he was with her now, and she was grateful.

"Here, why don't you try?" Jamie said, as if reading her mind. "Jest take these in your hands like this." He showed her. "Now the most important thing is, don't pull back unless you want to stop. Daisy'll keep going pretty much on her own."

Frankie wasn't sure she believed that, but she focused on holding the reins steady, even though her instinct was, in fact, to pull them back. They both pretended not to notice that her hands were shaking.

In an undertone, so they wouldn't be heard, Jamie showed her what to do with the reins if she wanted Daisy to turn, stop, or go faster. It sounded a lot easier than it felt. The cart hit a groove and dipped down, and Frankie dropped one of the reins. As she bent down to retrieve it, Jamie grabbed them both and pulled to signal Daisy to stop. They were at the gatehouse and a guard walked over and started joking with Jamie.

"Don' worrit, any. I'll be right back," Jamie told the guard. "I'se jest takin', ah, my cousin, down the path a ways."

Frankie kept her head down and pretended to be looking for something.

The guard said something about a patrol going out soon. "Be sure ye're back when they want the horses, or you'll be whipped."

"Yessir," Jamie said, "I will." And off they went.

Frankie sat up again and almost hugged him, but she stopped because she didn't want to attract attention. "Oh, Jamie, thank you so much. You saved me!"

Jamie grinned from ear to ear. "Happy to, miss! Ye'r Lady Ilayna's friend, so ye'r my friend, too." They only drove a few minutes more before he pulled over and handed her the reins. "I have to go back now, miss. D'ye think ye can handle 'er?"

"I'll do my best, Jamie," Frankie said. "I'll do just what you told me to do. Thank you for all your help!"

Jamie got down and headed back toward the fortress. The crowds had thinned out, but there were still a lot of people on the road. As she watched him go, Frankie saw Jamie hail a man on a horse heading toward the fortress. The man stopped and pulled him up, then spurred his horse forward.

Frankie took a deep breath and let it out. It was up to her now. She flicked the reins as Jamie had shown her, and Daisy started moving again. "Help me out here, Daisy," she whispered, "I don't know what I'm doing."

Frankie and Daisy plodded along. Frankie was afraid to let Daisy go faster than a walk, but with each stride away from the fortress, she felt a little better. They had already passed the place where Ilayna had pulled the cart over that morning. The forest was getting thicker on both sides of the road, so Frankie knew she didn't have too far to go to reach the turn-off for the cottage where she would say goodbye to her friends and go home through the portal. Even so, Frankie felt a cloud of fear hanging over her that she just couldn't shake.

It wasn't long before she found out why.

Frankie heard them before she could see them coming. She heard a shout from somewhere in the distance behind her, followed by the pounding of hoof beats coming closer, fast. Frankie tried to think about what she could do, but she couldn't seem to get her mind to work. Daisy, too, sensed the danger and stopped.

Frankie's mind was suddenly flooded with images of her worst fears: being captured and thrown in Janra's dungeon. Every voice in her head was screaming at her, but she finally shook them into silence. She knew what she had to do. She was afraid to try to make Daisy go faster and knew that the other horses would catch up anyway. She looked at the forest and a glimmer of an idea floated up. She wasn't far from the turn for the cottage and she might do better on foot. Maybe the horses wouldn't be able to follow her into the forest and she'd have a chance to lose them.

Frankie grabbed her backpack and jumped down from the cart. She gave Daisy a smack on her hindquarters and told her to run. As Daisy bolted off in a trot, Frankie started running toward the trees as fast as her legs would carry her.

❧ 17 ❧

A Confrontation

They were gaining on her. She heard them coming closer, thrashing through the underbrush behind her. She couldn't let them catch her. She ran faster.

The path was getting narrower and narrower, and she was having trouble following it. And now it seemed to fork up ahead. Which way to go? She wasn't sure. All she wanted to do was sit down and rest. But they were too close.

Frankie had gotten a good head start. She was well into the depths of the forest when she heard the patrol ride past, and it took some time before they picked up her trail, left their horses, and followed her on foot. They had entered the forest like an explosion, and that had spurred her on, faster. But she was getting tired, so tired. And she was afraid they were catching up.

Her breath came in ragged gasps, and she veered to the left at the fork. She just kept running, telling her feet to keep going, to follow the path, overgrown as it was. Her lungs felt like they were going to explode and her backpack, slung over her shoulder by its strap, kept getting heavier and heavier. She had almost dropped it several times. She'd already stripped off the cloak, because she kept catching the loose fabric on branches as she ran. She didn't need it for disguise anymore.

Frankie stumbled over a branch lying across the path.

"I will go on," she forced the words into her mind as she righted herself and moved on.

Even without her crystal headband, she saw a thin, orange wisp of energy float out from her forehead as the thought formed in her mind. Good. It was working. Keep those good thoughts going, Frankie, she thought. The energy billowed out around her again, and she felt a surge of confidence. She kept on running. She stumbled again on the overgrown path. She tucked, rolled, scrambled back up to her feet, and kept on running without missing a beat. Pretty good for someone who got a D in gym, she thought, but she understood now why her dad thought fitness was important!

If only she could find a place to hide, someplace to rest while her pursuers ran past. "Oh, please, somebody help me do this," she said out loud, remembering Aldebaran's promise that all she ever had to do was ask, and help would come. She hoped it would come in time.

She kept running, but suddenly she felt like hundreds of loving hands were helping her along, steadying her on the path. And she thought she heard voices murmuring among the trees: *You can do it. You're almost there. You can do it.*

Several arrows and a crystal spear whizzed past her head, as it to remind her that danger was not very far behind. They were getting too close!

I AM SAFE! She shrieked the thought into her mind, and saw a sweeping band of silver light form a protective column around her. She knew it would stay there as long as she believed in it. But fear could dissolve it, and she was full of fear. She had to keep going. She had to get through the door between the two worlds and lock it before they could come through behind her.

She felt like her lungs were about to collapse, and the pain in her legs and side was excruciating. She wanted to stop and lie down. Just for a minute. To rest quietly one more time in these magical woods, breathing in the calm energy of those great wise trees. But she had to keep going.

She knew that the cottage couldn't be much farther, so she tucked her head and kept running. She could hear her pursuers getting closer. She could hear them gasping for breath, as she was. And she could hear them shouting to each other. Then she heard the one voice that she didn't want to hear: Janra! She almost fell when she realized that Janra was there, behind her, but she steadied herself and kept running.

A movement to the right caught her eye: there was something just out of her line of vision. She could hear someone, or something, crunching the leaves and gravel underfoot. This was a new sound . . it seemed like. . . just possibly. . . YES! She turned her head a bit more and saw the golden glint of the horn.

Aldebaran, his white silken mane streaming and his golden horn shining, galloped along with her, not ten feet from her side. He wasn't completely visible, but he was there.

I have been here, with you, the words drifted softly into her mind, *I was always nearby, but you could not see me. You have done well, my dear one, and I am very proud.*

She was happy to see him now, but sad to know it would be the last time. She wouldn't even have time to say good-bye. With her pursuers so close, she couldn't stop. She had to keep running — to the cottage, to the portrait, to her own world and her grandfather's house. But he was here now, cheering her along. And his words gave her new strength and determination. She *had* done well! And she was proud of herself.

Her chin raised up just a bit and she drew in a deep breath. She could make it now. She had to, and she would. She would get to the cottage and go through the portal and lock it shut.

She would make sure that Janra would never get through the door between the worlds. Aldebaran was counting on her to do that. More important, *she* was counting on herself to do that. It was her road. And she *could* travel it.

She could just make out the outline of the cottage through the trees, and she could almost feel the hot breath of her pursuers on the back of her neck. The beautiful garnet bracelet from Ilayna fairly leaped from her arm, as if it sacrificed itself to keep one attacker from getting a firm grip on Frankie's wrist. He tripped and fell as she ran ahead. She'd lost the necklace that Uriel gave her when she stumbled and caught it on a branch. And her amethyst earrings had fallen off somewhere along the way. She still had her headband in her backpack, but all her other wonderful presents were gone. But she didn't have time to think about that right now.

Frankie gave a final, desperate lunge, cleared the trees, and sprinted the last few hundred yards onto the grass in front of the cottage. She was here. She had made it. And, suddenly, she was mad. She was tired, she was in pain, and she was *mad*. She felt that all her life she had been scared and insecure and bullied by other people. And now, quite simply and quite suddenly, she had had enough.

Frankie could feel rage and rebellion rise up inside her as the fear somehow drained away. She had been mugged, grabbed, kidnapped, thrown into a boat, taken to a fortress, intimidated, locked up, threatened and chased. And she had just had to take it. She hadn't been able to talk back or fight back. She had never had the courage to stand up for herself and fight back. Not really. She had always been too afraid of what she might lose if she did: her allowance, her friends, a good grade in class, or whatever. And now, finally, she was going to say something, do something, on her own behalf. She was going to stand up and speak her mind. Even though—this time—she had *everything* to lose.

Without quite knowing why, she spun around on her heel, held her right hand straight out in front of her with her palm up facing Janra, who was across the clearing with her men, and ordered "*STOP!*"

And for some reason, Janra did. They all did. Janra and all her men. They all just stopped. In their tracks. As if the force of the energy from Frankie's outstretched hand had stopped them like a brick wall.

Frankie looked behind Janra and was astonished at the number of warriors she had brought to catch just one young girl. On the other side of the clearing, she was also surprised to see Uriel and Unarius standing with Aradia and Ilayna, with Aradia's blue-uniformed men stepping forward to hold Janra's men at bay. Ilayna started to move toward Frankie, then shook her head slightly and stopped, giving her a smile, instead.

Janra looked like she was being held back by strong, invisible hands, and Frankie could almost hear the thoughts going through her head as she struggled to break free. Janra's rage and frustration formed a huge dark storm cloud that spread over the entire clearing, and little red and orange arrows shot around in it. Even without her headband, Frankie could see it.

"I don't like you, Janra," Frankie said. "You think you can just push people around and make them do whatever you say. But you can't do that anymore. People have rights, you know, and you can't just go on ignoring that. You're just a big nasty bully, and I've just had it with you! I've had it with all the bullies!" As she said it, Frankie pointed emphatically at the woman. "You have to stop it, do you hear me? You have to stop pushing people around. JUST STOP IT! NOW!"

She suddenly felt the planet's energy rise up inside her, like warm electricity, up her legs, through her body and down her arm. It was a great surge of power, filling her and making her strong. And she was more flabbergasted than anyone when bright purple lightning streamed out from her fingertips, leaped across the clearing and hit Janra's arm, singeing it in a black smoldering line from shoulder to wrist.

For a moment, time stopped. Nothing moved and nobody breathed. Then Frankie broke the spell. She spun back around, clutched her precious backpack against her shoulder, and ran toward the cottage. Pandemonium broke loose in the small clearing behind her.

As she loped up onto the front porch and in through the door, she heard the hubbub in her wake. Voices shouted in wild confusion. Janra shrieked, "Get her! Stop her!" And someone else hollered "Stop Janra."

Before she had time to think about what was happening, Frankie clutched her backpack against her stomach and dived head first into the large portrait on the wall. She had just enough time to hope that the door between worlds was still open, before she fell into that sickening void. She floated down through the cold fog, her insides churning, for what seemed like eternity.

Suddenly, her shoulders struck something hard, she tucked herself into a ball, and she rolled. There was silence for a moment and Frankie took in the blue rug, the big mahogany bed, and the pineapple-topped poles of the old carved cheval mirror that told her without a doubt that she was back in her Aunt Cassie's room. Then she heard Janra's shrieking voice, as the portal opened again behind her.

"Oh my gosh!" Frankie gasped and scrambled to her feet.

Janra's head, shoulders, and that one singed arm were actually moving into the room through the portrait as Frankie pulled the double-terminated crystal key from her backpack and jammed it into the hole on the base of the frame. Janra disappeared so suddenly that Frankie collapsed on the floor in astonishment and relief. Her legs just gave out from under her.

Frankie scrambled away and sat back, leaning against the sideboard of the bed. She stared at the large portrait of Cybele on the wall—the picture she had just fallen through. Her breath was still coming in gasps as she watched the picture change before her eyes, just as it had at the beginning of her journey into Alaris. First, she saw Cybele standing in her buckskins on the cottage porch, smiling as she watched Aradia being lifted up and cheered by her own men and Janra's men. A few men pulled an unconscious Janra out of the cottage. Frankie thought she caught a glint of silvery white mane and golden horn just inside the woods at the edge of the clearing.

Then the picture blurred and shifted, and Frankie could see Aradia and Ilayna riding toward the gatehouse of Kelghard, with all the warriors behind them. The banners from the tournament lined the road, adding a festive flair, and the people along the way were cheering.

The picture unfocused and changed one more time, and when it resettled, Cybele was back as before, shown larger than life from the waist up, with just the hint of a tree or two behind her. She was smiling.

Frankie felt something reach out and caress her cheek, and she smiled back. She unzipped the pocket of her backpack, removed the pink heart-shaped stone, and carefully put it back in its place on the big wooden picture frame. Rose quartz, carrying the energy of love, Unarius had said. Love is the key. Frankie sighed.

Satisfied that the portal was finally closed and locked for good, she reached into her backpack and pulled out the shard of crystal that still held part of Aunt Cassie. She stood up and threw the crystal shard onto the floor as hard as she could. It smashed to smithereens, and Frankie was sure she heard a deep, happy chuckle as wispy peach-colored vapor spiraled into the air and out into the hall. She'd know in a minute if it had really worked. A moment later, she heard a familiar laugh rumble back down the hall toward her—it was her Aunt Cassie's laugh—like it used to be, filled with gusto and joy.

Frankie surveyed herself in the big carved mirror in the corner. She looked the same as she looked when she left. How long had it been? She must have been gone at least six months. She looked down at the bed and noticed the stack of coats and purses, a blue and white diaper bag, a red toy car. She recognized her blue coat, the new one she had gotten when the weather turned cold last month. And she recognized her brother's small plaid jacket.

And slowly it dawned on her: Could it be that she had really returned to the exact same time when she had left? Aldebaran had assured her that she didn't have to worry about time, because she crossed time and space when she walked through the door between the worlds. She'd always wanted to believe him, but she didn't realize until now that she really *hadn't* believed it. Now she wasn't so sure. Stranger things had happened to her, after all, and Frankie wasn't about to start doubting her senses now. A person who has walked through a portrait into another world, who has lived there, fought there, saved her world from an enemy invasion, and insulted the Mistress of All the Worlds wouldn't really quibble over a strange concept in time. She looked at the calendar and clock on the night stand: the date was the same, and the clock said 7:10 p.m. She'd only been gone about four minutes!

Frankie looked in the mirror again. She had changed so much during her visit to Alaris. She had learned new things, challenged herself in ways she had never imagined, and gained a new sense of self-confidence and self-respect. But she looked just the same as before. That might make it easier for her, though. If all those changes didn't show on the outside, she might just be able to hide them. But Frankie knew she would never, ever, see, or do, or feel things in quite the same way again. And she wasn't exactly sure whether that was good or bad. If other people noticed the changes in her, how would she ever explain? Maybe that would be *their* problem?

She pulled her Aunt's necklace out of her backpack and slipped it into Aunt Cassie's handbag on the bed. Then she walked out into the hall. She paused and listened to the sounds in the house, waiting as Unarius had taught her, until each noise settled into its own identifiable space. She heard someone puttering around in the kitchen — probably Grandma putting the dishes into the dishwasher. She heard her Dad's voice in the den, arguing with someone about politics again. And she heard the kids playing and screaming downstairs — no mistaking those sounds!

Frankie made herself stand there at the end of the long, carpeted hallway, forcing herself not to run into the kitchen screaming, "Here I am! Here I am! I'm back! I'm safe!" That was what she felt like doing, but she knew her family would think she was crazy. After all, they didn't even know she'd been gone!

Frankie walked down the hall slowly, one foot in front of the other, holding herself back, trying to contain her excitement. She walked up to the door of the den, where she could hear everybody talking over the roar of the football game on television. She liked her family, especially at times like this, when they filled her granddad's den and sat in the warm glow of a fire, talking, arguing, and laughing. Frankie walked in, stood in the doorway, and waited for a reaction.

No one said anything. Not for a minute, anyway.

Her eyes found Aunt Cassie, who was sitting on the sofa across the room, apparently in deep conversation with Aunt Meg. She looked like the old Aunt Cassie, before she got sick. A healthy glow had replaced the pale pallor on her face. Frankie sent up a silent little prayer of thanks.

Aunt Cassie looked up, looked Frankie straight in the eye,

put her forefinger up to her grinning lips for a moment, and winked. She gave a quick "thumbs up" gesture and then turned back to Aunt Meg, adding something to the give and take of conversation. And Frankie would have sworn she saw the faintest little wisp of pink energy come swirling across the room to her.

Lost in the feel of that small pink wisp—and astonishment that she could see it here, without her headband—Frankie almost jumped out of her skin when her father spoke from the depths of the green velvet wing chair across the room: "Frankie, what have you been up to? You're all scruffy. You haven't been up in the attic have you? I told you not to go up there. Don't you ever listen?"

"Don't worry, Dad, I haven't been up in the attic," Frankie said to her father, forcing herself to walk casually across the room instead of catapulting to his side. She was surprised that she could see a dark brownish-red cloud floating around his head, and she knew what that meant. Even without her headband she could see that it was pretty thick and dark.

She realized suddenly that things hadn't been easy for him, either, since her mother died. She had been so overwhelmed by her own pain that she hadn't been able to see what he was going through. She also realized that his chiding remarks and criticisms weren't going to hurt her anymore the way they once did. Now she could see how hard it was for him, and she knew he was doing his best, trying to be both parents. Besides, she had much more confidence in herself now. She didn't need him to tell her that she had value—she knew it, deep inside. She gave him a big hug, suddenly aware of how much she had missed him.

"I've just been in the guest room, looking at all the stuff," she told him, crossing her fingers behind her back because of her white lie, "I guess I got a little dusty. That's all. You don't have to worry about me, Dad. I'm fine. Really."

He gave her an awkward hug back and looked at her quizzically. He had expected her usual defensive response and he was surprised at her gesture of affection. He softened. "Well, Frankie," he said with a sort of grumbling hoarseness, as if he wanted to say something but didn't quite know how, "I don't mean to give you a hard time, you know. It's just that I do worry about you. I guess I've been worrying a lot lately, and sometimes I snap at you when I don't really mean to. It's hard trying to be both mom and dad. Don't take it to heart, okay honey?"

"I know, Dad," she said. "I won't." And she knew that she really wouldn't.

Aunt Cassie casually yawned and stretched and got up from the couch across the room. She walked over and put an arm around Frankie and a hand on her brother's shoulder. "It's nice to see you two talking nicely again. That bellow of yours, Tom, gets old pretty fast, you know."

"Yeah, well," Tom Maxwell muttered into his chest, giving Frankie's arm a squeeze. "You know, Cass," he added, changing the subject as he looked up at his sister, "you look better than I've seen you in a long time. Taking the last few months off from work has really done you some good. You look really rested, now, and sort of back to normal."

"I know, Tom," Aunt Cassie answered, "I feel like myself again for the first time in years. Literally. It's good to be back." She patted his shoulder, and then squeezed Frankie's. "Come into the dining room and play cards with me, Frankie. I'm bored with football and I think you owe me a rematch. Besides, I want to hear about what you've been up to lately."

Frankie could hardly contain herself, but she tried to act just as nonchalant as her aunt. "Sure, Aunt Cassie. But I bet I can beat you!"

When they reached the living room, Frankie threw herself into her aunt's arms.

"I went to Alaris! I really did! I was there!" she whispered triumphantly, all in one big rush. "And the minute I saw that peach-colored crystal, I just *knew* it was you! And I got kidnapped, and I got rescued, and I met a unicorn—his name is Aldebaran, and I think you know him, too—and I went into the fortress and took back the crystals, and I zapped Janra with lightening! I did it myself! I can hardly believe it!"

"I believe it," Aunt Cassie agreed. "As soon as I realized what had happened—and where you'd gone—I was absolutely certain you'd succeed," she said, easing out of her embrace to look Frankie in the eye.

"How did you know?" Frankie asked, still breathless.

Aunt Cassie tapped Frankie on the chest, right over her heart. "I knew because you found the door between the worlds, and that didn't just happen by accident. Cybele must have called you and let you in."

"That's right," Frankie said, remembering how the portrait had changed, as if the woman were calling her to come.

"And Cybele wouldn't have called you if you weren't supposed to go, if there wasn't something for you to do there."

"Like it was part of my path to go," Frankie added. "But how did you know I'd be okay?"

Cassie ruffled Frankie's hair and chuckle. "Because, my dear, I have great faith in you. I know that you have all the strength and wisdom you'll ever need right there inside you, and..."

"All you have to do is learn to listen!" they both said in unison.

And then they both started laughing, as they heard a faint—but unmistakable—"I told you so" unicorn snort.

Acknowledgments

A number of people have held the vision of this book for a long time, offering unwavering friendship, support, and encouragement, even when I lost faith. For that, I am particularly grateful to Jane Batt, Elisabeth Fitzhugh, and LouEllen Murphy Rice. As if total faith and unflagging support weren't enough, I also thank Jane for sharing her insights about life and her expertise about children's books; LouEllen, for sharing my path for so many years: the best of friends and a life line when I felt adrift; and Elisabeth, for unfailing mentoring and hand-holding before and during the publication process, and for bringing to the world, and to me, ORION, beloved friends and teachers (www.orionwisdom.org), whose wisdom and humor enrich these pages.

Several others also came into my life and offered assistance when I needed it. For that, I thank Debra Daniel for her ongoing friendship, wise counsel, and generous nature; Frances Smokowski and Mary Beth O'Quinn for insightful editorial comments; and Jonathan Horstman for his beautiful map of Alaris and Kelghard.

And, of course, special thanks to Emily, who started it all when she asked me to write her a story!

About the Author

Ellyn Dye has had many incarnations. She has been an actress, a folksinger, a photographer, a writer, an editor, a director of communications, an energy worker, and "staff" for a succession of cats. She has worked for a theater, a labor union, several trade associations, a medical association, the YMCA, and federal and local government. Over thirty years of metaphysical studies and mystical experiences—and a full-fledged Near Death Experience—inform and enrich her world view and her writing.

Ellyn travels widely, favoring places with mystical/spiritual associations, and she has a particular interest in the so-called Indigo children (also called the *new* or *psychic* children). This is Ellyn's first novel, and it was written for Indigo children of all ages. You know who you are!

Made in the USA